AS THE PIG TURNS

AN AGATHA RAISIN MYSTERY

AS THE PIG TURNS

M. C. BEATON

**THORNDIKE
CHIVERS**

LIBRARY OF CONGRESS CATALOGING-IN-PUBLICATION DATA

Beaton, M. C.
    As the pig turns : an Agatha Raisin mystery / by M. C. Beaton.
      p. cm. — (Thorndike Press large print mystery)
    ISBN-13: 978-1-4104-4110-2 (hardcover)
    ISBN-10: 1-4104-4110-5 (hardcover)
    1. Raisin, Agatha (Fictitious character)—Fiction. 2. Women private investigators—England—Cotswold Hills—Fiction. 3. Police—Crimes against—Fiction. 4. Cotswold Hills (England)—Fiction. 5. Large type books. I. Title.
    PR6053.H4535A85 2011b
    823'.914—dc22   2011031068

BRITISH LIBRARY CATALOGUING-IN-PUBLICATION DATA AVAILABLE
Published in the U.S. in 2011 by arrangement with St. Martin's Press, LLC.
Published in the U.K. in 2012 by arrangement with Constable & Robinson Ltd.
U.K. Hardcover: 978 1 445 86554 6 (Chivers Large Print)
U.K. Softcover: 978 1 445 86555 3 (Camden Large Print)

Printed and bound in Great Britain by the MPG Books Group
1 2 3 4 5 6 7 15 14 13 12 11

This book is dedicated to Sinead Goss, with many thanks for all her support for Target Ovarian Cancer.

CHAPTER ONE

Agatha Raisin wearily turned onto the road leading down into her home village of Carsely in the Cotswolds and then came to an abrupt halt. Cars stretched out in front of her. She pulled on the handbrake.

It was the end of January and a very cold month, unusually cold. The tall trees on either side of the country road raised bare branches to a leaden sky as if pleading for the return of spring. Agatha prayed it would not snow. It seemed as if two centimetres of snow were enough to close down the roads, because the council complained they had run out of salt and all roads leading out of Carsely were very steep, making driving hazardous.

What on earth was going on? She gave an impatient blast on her horn, and the young man in the battered Ford in front gave her the finger.

Cursing, Agatha got out of her car and

marched up to the Ford and rapped on the window. The sallow-faced youth opened the window and demanded, "Wot?"

"What the hell's going on?" demanded Agatha.

The youth eyed her up and down, noting the expensively tailored coat and the beady, accusing eyes and marking the "posh" accent. He scowled. "Pot'oles," he said with a shrug. "They're repairing pot'oles."

"And how long will it take?"

"Blessed if I know," he said, and rolled up the window.

Agatha returned to the warmth of her car, fuming. She herself had complained bitterly to the council about the state of the road. But there were two other roads into the village. They might at least have put up diversion notices until the road was repaired. She contemplated making a U-turn but knew, considering her lack of driving skills, it would take her an awful lot of manoeuvring on the narrow road to do so.

A drip began to appear on the end of her nose. She reached into the box of tissues on the seat beside her and blew her nose. Someone rapped at the window.

Agatha looked out. A policeman was bending down looking at her. He was squat and burly, with a squashed-looking nose in his open-pored face and piggy, accusing little eyes.

Lowering the window, Agatha asked, "How long is this going to take, Officer?"

"It'll take as long as it takes, madam," he said in a thick Gloucestershire accent. "I am ticketing you for taking your hands off the wheel."

"My, what? Are you mad? I was simply blowing my nose. The handbrake's on, I'm stuck here . . ."

"Sixty-pound fine."

"I'll see you in hell first before I pay that," howled Agatha.

He handed in a ticket. "See you in court."

Agatha sat for a moment, shaking with rage. Then she took a deep breath. She started to negotiate a U-turn, but cars piled up behind her had decided to do the same thing. At last she was clear, just in time to see in her rearview mirror that the line of cars she had just left had started to move.

By the time she reached her thatched cottage in Lilac Lane, it had begun to snow, fine little pellets of snow. Damn all pundits and their moaning about global warming, thought Agatha. As she opened the car door to get out, a gust of wind whipped the ticket the policeman had given her and sent it flying up over her cottage.

9

She let herself into her cottage. Her two cats, Hodge and Boswell, came running forward to give her the welcome they always gave her when they wanted something to eat.

Agatha fed them, poured herself a gin and tonic, and then phoned her friend Detective Sergeant Bill Wong. When he came on the phone, Agatha complained bitterly about the policeman who had given her a ticket for blowing her nose.

"That would be Gary Beech," said Bill, "the target fiend. You know we have to meet certain targets or we don't get promotion. He goes a bit mad. The other week, a nine-year-old's mother who lives in a cul-de-sac in Mircester chalked squares on the pavement for her little boy to play hopscotch. Beech arrested the kid and charged him with the crime of graffiti. And he charged a toddler with carrying a dangerous weapon even though the kid was holding a water pistol. An old-age pensioner was arrested under the Terrorism Act for carrying a placard saying, 'Get our boys out of Afghanistan.' "

"What should I do?"

"It'll probably be thrown out of court. Or you could just pay the fine."

"Never!"

"How's business?"

"Not good. The recession is really biting. People just don't have the money." Agatha looked out of her kitchen window. "Blast! The snow's getting thicker. I wish I'd invested in snow tyres or a four-wheel drive. Roy Silver's coming down for the week-end. I hope the roads clear by then."

Roy had worked for Agatha when she had run a successful public relations business in London. She had taken early retirement and had sold up to move to the Cotswolds. But after solving several murders, she had decided to set up her own detective agency.

Bill said he would try to get down to see her at the week-end and rang off.

Agatha then phoned her agency. She had a small staff: Patrick Mulligan, a retired policeman, Phil Marshall, an elderly man from Carsely, young Toni Gilmour and a secretary, Mrs. Freedman. A shrewd businesswoman, Agatha had seen the recession coming long before most people and so had decided not to employ any more staff. But there was one absence from her staff jabbing at her conscience. A bright young detective, Simon Black, employed by Agatha until a few months earlier, had shown signs of falling in love with Toni. Persuading herself that she was acting in their best interests, Agatha had told Simon that Toni was too young and to wait three years. But Toni had turned against Simon, feeling he was snubbing her at every turn, and to Agatha's horror, Simon had gone off and enlisted in the army and was now fighting in Afghanistan.

Toni answered the phone and said that Mrs. Freedman and Phil had gone home, not wanting to wait any longer in case the snow got thicker. Toni, young, blond and beautiful, often gave Agatha pangs of envy, but she had to admit that the girl was a brilliant detective.

"What have we got outstanding?" asked Agatha.

"Two adulteries, four missing pets and two missing teenagers."

Agatha sighed. "It seems not so long ago that I swore I would never take on another missing pet. Now we need the money."

"It's easy money," said Toni. "They hardly ever think of checking the animal shelter. I just go along there with the photos they've given me of Tiddles or whatever, collect the beasts and phone the happy owners and then say, 'Pay up.' "

"Roy's coming down for the week-end," said Agatha, "and maybe Bill will come over. Why don't you join us and maybe I'll

12

find something interesting for us to do?"

"I've got a date."

"Who is he?"

"Paul Finlay."

"How did you meet him?"

Toni longed to tell the ever-curious Agatha to mind her own business, but she said reluctantly, "I've been taking French classes in the evenings, now that it's quiet at work. He's the lecturer."

"How old is he?"

"I've got to go. The other phone's ringing."

After she had rung off, Agatha sat and worried. Toni had a weakness for older men and had run into trouble before.

Agatha's cleaner, Doris Simpson, had left a local newspaper on the kitchen table. She began to search through it to see if there were any week-end amusements, and then her eye fell on an event in Winter Parva, a village some twenty miles away. Agatha had been to Winter Parva only once. It was a touristy Cotswold village with gift shops, a mediaeval market hall and thatched cottages. The article said that as the local shops had not fared as well as usual over the Christmas period, the parish council had planned to generate interest in the village with a special January event. There was to be a pig roast on Saturday on the village green. The villagers were urged to dress in old-fashioned costumes. The Winter Parva morris dancers would perform along with the local brass band and the village choir. Two busloads of Chinese tourists were expected to arrive for the event.

That'll do, thought Agatha, as long as I'm not blocked in the village by the snow.

Feeling hungry, she rummaged in her deep freezer to find something to micro-wave. Suddenly all the lights went out. A power cut.

She remembered the pub, the Red Lion, had a generator. Agatha changed into trousers, boots and a hooded parka and set out in the hunt for dinner.

The pub was crowded with locals. Agatha went to the bar and ordered lasagne and chips and a half of lager and looked around for a vacant table. Then, to her amazement, she saw her friend the vicar's wife, Mrs. Bloxby, sitting by herself in a corner, looking down dismally at a small glass of sherry.

Agatha hurried to join her, wondering what could be wrong, because Mrs. Bloxby never went to the pub unless it was some special fund-raising occasion. The vicar's wife had grey hair escaping from an old-fashioned bun. Her normally kind face looked tired. She was wearing a shabby tweed coat over a washed-out sweater, cardigan and tweed skirt. It didn't matter what she wore, thought Agatha, not for the first time. Mrs. Bloxby always had "lady" stamped on her. Agatha and Mrs. Bloxby always called each other by their second names, a tradition in the local Ladies Society, of which both were members.

"How odd to see you here," said Agatha. "Where's your husband?"

"I neither know nor care," said Mrs. Bloxby. "Do sit down, Mrs. Raisin."

Agatha sat down opposite her. "What is the matter?"

Mrs. Bloxby seemed to rally. She gave a weak smile. "It's nothing, really. Do you really mean to eat that?"

The waitress had placed a dish of lasagne and chips in front of Agatha. "Sure. What's up with it?" Agatha dug her fork in and took a mouthful.

Mrs. Bloxby reflected that her friend had the taste buds of a vulture.

Yet Agatha sometimes managed to make her feel diminished. Although in her early fifties, Agatha glowed with health, and her glossy brown hair, although expertly dyed, gleamed like silk.

"It can't be nothing," said Agatha, reaching for the ketchup bottle, opening it and dousing her chips.

"Probably my imagination," said Mrs. Bloxby wearily.

"You always did have good instincts. Out with it," commanded Agatha.

Mrs. Bloxby gave a heart-wrenching dry sob, the kind a child gives after crying for a long time. "It's just that I think Alf is having an affair. You're dribbling ketchup."

"Oh, sorry." Agatha put a chip, overloaded with ketchup, back on her plate. "Your husband is having an affair? Rubbish!"

"You're right. I'm just being silly."

"No, no, I shouldn't have said that. I mean, who would want him?" remarked Agatha with her usual lack of tact.

Her friend bristled. "I will have you know that as vicar of this parish, Alf has often been the target of predatory ladies."

"So what makes you think he's having an affair? Lipstick on his dog collar?"

"Nothing like that. It's just that he's taken to sneaking off without his dog collar on and he won't tell me where he's going."

"Been buying any new underwear recently?"

"No, I buy his underwear."

"Look, I'll find out for you and put your mind at rest. On the house."

16

"Oh, don't do that. If he saw you tailing him, he would be furious."

"He won't see me. I happen to be a very good detective."

"You are to do nothing about it," said Mrs. Bloxby seriously. "Promise?"

"Promise," agreed Agatha, and surreptitiously and childishly crossed her fingers behind her back.

A warm wind from the west during the night melted the snow to slush, and then, when the wind changed round to the north, it froze the roads into skating rinks. Agatha awoke the next day in a bad temper. How on earth was she going to get out of the village? It seemed small consolation that the power was back on.

But as she was having her usual breakfast of black coffee and cigarettes, she faintly heard a sound from the end of the lane, a sound she had not heard for some time. She put on her boots and coat and ran to the end of the lane. A gritter was making its lumbering way down through the village, spraying the road with grit and salt.

Agatha hurried back to put on her make-up and get dressed for the office.

She was just driving out of Lilac Lane when she recognised the vicar's car on the road ahead of her. "Just a little look wouldn't hurt," she assured herself. She let the car behind her pass her and then followed, keeping the vicar's car in view. He drove to the nearby village of Ancombe and parked in the courtyard of St. Mary's, a large Catholic church. The village of Ancombe had remained loyal to Charles I when all about, the Puritans supported Cromwell.

Driven by curiosity, Agatha parked out on the road and went up the drive past the gravestones and into the church.

In the dimness of the church, she could just make out the thin figure of Mr. Bloxby going into a confessional box and closing the door. She ducked down in a pew as a priest appeared and went into the confessional.

I must know what he is saying, fretted Agatha. She took off her shoes and tiptoed towards the confessional box into which the vicar had disappeared, put her ear against it and listened hard.

"What do you think you are doing?" roared a stentorian voice.

Agatha caught a frightened glimpse of a man who had just entered the church. She quickly closed her eyes and slumped to the floor. The confessional opened and Mr.

18

Bloxby and the priest came out.

"What is going on?" demanded the reedy voice of the priest.

Agatha opened her eyes. "What happened?" she demanded weakly. "I felt dizzy and saw Mr. Bloxby coming in here and wanted to ask him for help."

"She was listening!" said a thin, acidulous man.

"I know this woman," said Mr. Bloxby. "Mrs. Raisin, step outside the church with me."

Agatha got to her feet. No one helped her. She put on her shoes. Mr. Bloxby marched ahead, and Agatha trailed after him, miserably.

Outside the church, Mr. Bloxby snapped, "Get in my car, Mrs. Raisin. You have some explaining to do."

Agatha got into the passenger seat of the vicar's car. It had begun to rain: soft, weeping rain.

"Now," said Mr. Bloxby, "explain yourself, you horrible woman." The vicar had never liked Agatha and could not understand his wife's affection for her.

She'll never speak to me again, thought Agatha sadly as she realised she would have to tell the truth.

"It's like this, Alf . . . may I call you Alf?"

"No."

"Okay, what happened, I met your wife in the pub last night and she had been crying. She thinks you're having an affair."

"How ridiculous . . . although come to think of it, I have had to ward off a few amorous parishioners over the years."

"I promised not to snoop," said Agatha.

"Which in your case is like promising not to breathe."

"Right! I'm fed up feeling guilty," said Agatha. "What the hell were you doing in the confessional box of a Catholic church?"

"I needed spiritual guidance."

"Don't tell me you've lost your faith?" demanded Agatha.

"Nothing like that. You know that we use the old Book of Common Prayer and the King James Bible?"

Agatha hadn't noticed, but she said, "Yes."

"It is the most beautiful writing, on a par with Shakespeare. The bishop has ordered me to change to modern translations of both. I can't, I just can't. I felt I had to unburden myself to a priest of a different faith."

"Why on earth didn't you tell your wife?"

"I had to wrestle with my conscience. I even thought of entering the Catholic Church."

"And taking a vow of celibacy?"

"The Vatican is proposing making provisions for people like myself."

"Don't you *talk* to your wife?"

"I prefer to wrestle with spiritual matters on my own."

Agatha saw a way out of her predicament. She threw him a cunning look out of her small, bearlike eyes. "I could fix it for you."

"You! Do me a favour."

"I will, if you'll shut up and listen. The bishop will not go against the wishes of the parishioners. The whole village will sign a petition to keep things as they are and send it to the bishop. Easy. I'll fix it for you if you promise not to tell Mrs. Bloxby I had anything to do with it. I'll fix it up with the local shop. Everyone shops there in the bad weather. I'll get Mrs. Tutchell, the new owner, to say it's her idea. You start talking about it now, all round the village, starting with your wife. Of course, if I find you have breathed a word about my involvement in this, you're on your own, mate. Of all the silly vicars . . ."

"Why didn't you tell me before?" asked Mrs. Bloxby plaintively half an hour later, after having heard her husband's explanation.

"At first, I wanted to wrestle with the problem on my own, but I called in at the village store and happened to mention it on my way home. The villagers have been very supportive and are sending a petition to the bishop."

"Did Mrs. Raisin have anything to do with this?"

"Of course not," said the vicar, addressing the sitting room fire. Just a white lie, God, he assured his Maker. "Can you imagine me asking her for help?"

Agatha busied herself for most of the rest of the day by going door-to-door in the village, raising support for the vicar and urging everyone to sign the petition at the village store. A good proportion of the villagers were incomers who only went to church at Easter and Christmas but were anxious to do the right "village thingie," as one overweight matron put it. Agatha headed to the office in the late afternoon to find Toni just leaving on the arm of a tall, tweedy man who sported a beard.

"This is Paul Finlay," said Toni.

"Ah, the great detective," said Paul. He was in his late thirties, Agatha guessed, with an infuriatingly patronising air. He had a craggy face and the sort of twinkling humorous eyes that belie the fact that the owner has no sense of humour whatsoever.

"We're off out for the evening," said Toni quickly. "Bye."

"Wait a bit," said Agatha. "Roy's coming on Friday night, and on Saturday, we're going to a pig roast in Winter Parva. Why don't you and Paul come along? Come to my cottage and I'll take you over because the parking's going to be awful."

"A pig roast?" cackled Paul. "How quaint. Of course we'll come."

"Good. The pig roast starts at six, but I'd like to get there a bit earlier," said Agatha. "See you around four o'clock for drinks and then we'll all go."

Agatha stood and watched them as they walked away. Toni's slim young figure looked dwarfed and vulnerable beside the tall figure of Paul.

"Not suitable at all. What a prick," said Agatha, and a passing woman gave her a nervous look.

Agatha checked business in the office before heading home again. She was just approaching Lilac Lane when a police car swung in front of her, blocking her.

Agatha jammed on the brakes and looked in her rearview mirror. She saw the lumbering figure of the policeman who had ticketed her for blowing her nose. She rolled down the window as he approached. "Now what?" she demanded.

"I had a speed camera in me 'and up in that there road," he said, "and you was doing thirty-two miles an hour. So that's three points off your licence and a speeding fine."

Agatha opened her mouth to blast him but quickly realised he would probably fine her for abusing a police officer. He proceeded to give her a lecture on the dangers of speeding, and Agatha knew he was trying to get her to lose her temper, so she listened quietly until he gave up.

When he had finally gone, she swung the car round and went into the village store, where she informed an interested audience about the iniquities of the police in general and one policeman in particular. "I'd like to kill him," she shouted. "May he roast slowly over a spit in hell."

It was a frosty Friday evening when Agatha met Roy Silver at Moreton-in-Marsh station. He was dressed in black trousers and a black sweater, over which he was wearing a scarlet jacket with little flecks of gold in the weave. He had shaved his head bald, and Agatha thought dismally that her friend looked like a cross between a plucked chicken and someone auditioning for a job as a Red Coat entertainer at a Butlin's Holiday camp.

"Turn on the heater," said Roy as he got in the car. "I'm freezing."

"I'm not surprised," said Agatha. "What's with the bald head?"

"It's fashionable," said Roy petulantly, "and it strengthens the hair. It's only temporary."

"I'll lend you some warm clothes," said Agatha.

"Your clothes on me, babes?" said Roy waspishly. "I'd look as if I were wearing a tent. I mean, you could put two of me inside one of you."

"I'm not fat," snarled Agatha. "You're unhealthily thin. Charles has left some of his clothes in the spare room." Sir Charles Fraith, a friend of Agatha's, often used her cottage as a hotel.

Roy said mutinously that his clothes were perfectly adequate, but when they got to Agatha's cottage, they found there had been another power cut and the house was cold.

While Agatha lit the fire in her living room, Roy hung away his precious jacket in the wardrobe in the spare room, wondering how anyone could not love such a creation.

He found one of Charles's cashmere sweaters and put it on.

When he joined Agatha, the fire was blazing. "How long do these power cuts last?" he asked.

"Not long, usually," said Agatha. "There's something up with the power station that serves this end of the village."

"Anything planned for the week-end?"

"We're going to a pig roast at Winter Parva tomorrow."

"No use. I'm vegetarian."

"Since when?"

Roy looked shifty. "A month ago."

"You haven't been dieting. You've been starving yourself," accused Agatha. "I got steaks for dinner."

"Couldn't touch one," said Roy. "A pig roast? Do you mean turned on a spit like in those historical films?"

"Yes."

"Yuck, and double yucky, yucky yuck, Aggie. It'll be disgusting."

But the next day after Toni and Paul had arrived, and the erratic electricity had come on again, Roy decided that anything would be better than being left behind. Bill Wong had phoned to say he could not make it.

Just as they were having drinks, Charles

Fraith arrived. He was as expensively dressed as usual in smart casual clothes. He had small, neat features and well-barbered hair. Agatha never really knew what he thought of her. He helped himself to a whisky and then proceeded to put his foot in it. He asked Roy sympathetically if he had cancer. When Roy denied it, Charles said, "I was about to forgive you for wearing one of my sweaters, but as you aren't suffering, I do feel you might have asked me first."

"I told him he could borrow something," said Agatha. "I haven't introduced you to Paul Finlay."

"Toni's uncle?"

"No, just a friend," said Agatha.

Paul bristled. Charles's upper-class accent brought out the worst in him. His light Birmingham accent grew stronger as he suddenly treated them all to a rant about the unfairness of the British class system and about an aristocracy who lived on the backs of the poor.

Thank goodness for Charles, thought Agatha. Toni must see what a horror this man is.

But Toni was listening to Paul with shining eyes.

Charles waited until Paul had dried up,

said calmly, "What a lot of old-fashioned bollocks. When are we going?"

"Finish your drinks," said Agatha. "I want to be sure of getting a parking place. It'll be a bit of a crush in my car."

"I'll take Roy," said Charles.

"You'll need a coat," said Agatha to Roy. "You'll find my Barbour hanging in the hall. Use that."

"I could wear my jacket," said Roy.

"You'll freeze. Come along, everyone."

Thin trails of fog wound their way through the trees as they drove to Winter Parva. They had to park outside the village because all the parking places in the village had been taken. Paul, anxious to get Toni to himself, said they would look at the shops and meet the others on the village green in time for the pig roast.

Agatha, Charles and Roy walked to the nearest pub and into the grateful warmth of the bar.

"Something will need to be done about Paul," said Charles. "I think Toni's still a virgin, and the thought of her losing it under the hairy thighs of that bore is horrible."

"He might propose marriage," said Roy.

"I think I'll do a bit of detective work," said Agatha. "I bet he's either married or been married. Why can't Toni see what a bore he is? How can she listen to that class nonsense?"

"Maybe it strikes a chord," said Charles. "You forget, she was brought up rough. Maybe she doesn't know where she belongs in the scheme of things. There can be something very seductive about that sort of propaganda. Where the hell did she meet him?"

"At evening classes in French," said Agatha gloomily. "He's the lecturer."

Roy was looking round the bar at people dressed in mediaeval costume. "We could have dressed up, Aggie," he said plaintively.

Agatha looked at her watch. "I think we'd better make our way to the village green. I want to see how they prepare this pig."

The fog had thickened. If it hadn't been for the parked cars, you might have thought the village had reverted to the Middle Ages as the costumed villagers appeared and then disappeared in the fog.

Two men were bathing a huge pig in oil as it hung on a spit over a bed of blazing charcoal.

Some villagers were carrying flaming torches. As the fog lifted slightly, Agatha saw clearly on the haunch of the pig a tattoo of a heart with an arrow through it and the curly lettering "Amy." Her eyes flew down the length of the carcase to the chubby legs cut off above the knees.

"Stop!" she screamed at the top of her lungs.

The two men stopped turning the spit and stared at her. "Pigs don't have tattoos," said Agatha.

They peered at it. "Reckon someone's been 'aving a bit o' a joke," said one.

But Agatha had taken a powerful little torch out of her handbag and was examining the head.

"The head's been stitched on," she said. "Oh, God, I think this is the carcase of a man. Get the police."

CHAPTER TWO

Toni was cold and worried. She had wanted to join the others, but Paul had said he had something important to ask her. They had survived their first quarrel. They had argued because Toni refused to hear any criticism of Charles. Charles had been kind to her, she had protested. Paul fished in his pocket for the ring he had bought.

Then through the fog came the scream of police sirens. She heard a woman sob, "It's awful. Sick. Murder!"

She jumped to her feet. "Something's wrong. I've got to get to Agatha." Her slim figure in her bright red coat disappeared through the fog. Cursing under his breath, Paul got up and followed her.

Toni had to fight her way through a gathering crowd. Police were cordoning off the area around the pig roast. She elbowed her way to the front of the crowd. In the light of the fire and flaming torches held by some of the villagers, she saw Agatha, Charles and Roy being interviewed by Police Inspector Wilkes. Bill Wong stood beside him. Roy was standing behind them, busily telephoning.

Toni ducked under the tape. A policeman howled at her to get back, but Bill looked up and signalled it was all right to let her come through.

Paul tried to follow her, but a burly policeman barred his way. "I've got to get through," said Paul. "That's my fiancée over there."

"On the spit?" demanded the policeman.

"No, you idiot. The blond girl, there!"

"Did you call me an idiot?"

"No, no," said Paul weakly, backing off.

Agatha shivered as the questioning went on and on. She felt she was living in some Gothic horror movie. Her thoughts flew to her ex-husband. She hadn't seen him since the night he thought he had found Charles proposing to her. Actually, Charles *had* proposed to her until Agatha persuaded him that it wouldn't work, but Agatha, hearing James arriving, had quickly told Charles to get down on one knee and make it look real.

The macabre scene was suddenly lit up by white light. A television crew had arrived.

"Get a tent up round the body," snarled Wilkes. "Mrs. Raisin, I want you and your friends to go to police headquarters to make official statements. And that means you, too," he said, grabbing hold of Roy, who was about to duck under the tape and head for a television presenter.

Agatha said she would drive everybody there. She could just make out Paul shouting something from behind the tape but did not tell Toni.

After hours of further questioning at police headquarters, they all wearily signed their statements. Bill walked out with them to the reception.

Agatha drew him aside and whispered, "Do something for me. Toni's got a new squeeze called Paul Finlay, a lecturer at Mircester College, gives evening classes in French. He's too old for her. Could you look up the police files and see if there is anything on him?"

"I'll have my hands full with this case. Oh, don't glare at me. If I get a spare moment, I'll try."

Through the glass doors, Toni could see Paul waiting. "Coming back to my cottage with us?" asked Agatha.

Toni wanted to discuss the murder — if

murder it should turn out to be. Maybe someone had stolen a body from a grave or from a mortuary — and suddenly she did not want to see any more of Paul that evening.

"I'll join you there," she said. "Tell Paul I've gone home."

"Great! I mean, all right," said Agatha hurriedly.

Toni, familiar with the layout of police headquarters, left by the back door. She made her way slowly around to the front of the police station. There was no sign of Paul. She had left her car at Agatha's cottage, having driven Paul to Carsely. She assumed he had either got a lift in a police car or had taken a taxi to get to Mircester.

She saw a passing taxi and hailed it.

Agatha's cottage was besieged by press and television, Roy having phoned every branch of the media he could think of. Roy stood, grinning, next to Agatha, occasionally forgetting he was bald and tossing his head like a shampoo advertisement. When he later saw himself on television, he howled in dismay. He had a fatuous grin on his face, and his tossing head looked like a nervous twitch.

Agatha made a brief statement. Toni

shoved her way through the reporters. "Toni, Toni!" called several reporters, recognising the girl. "Give us a statement." Swinging round, Agatha fixed Toni with a baleful stare. Her beautiful detective hadn't even been there when the body was found, and she wasn't going to let her steal the limelight.

Toni nipped into the cottage, Agatha followed her and slammed the door. Roy and Charles were already in the living room. Charles had switched on the television.

"Turn that off!" ordered Agatha.

"But it's a rerun of *CSI Miami* on Sky," protested Charles. "Oh, suit yourself."

"Right," said Agatha. "We've got to solve this one."

"Can't do much until we know who the pig was," said Charles, stifling a yawn. "Bill interviewed you, Agatha. Did he tell you anything about what happened before we arrived on the scene?"

"No, but I overheard Wilkes interviewing the two men who operated the spit. They said two men dressed as knights carried the pig to the spit in a canvas sack. One of the spit operators, forget his name, he said the local butcher was supposed to bring it along in his van, but the knights said the butcher had thought if they dressed up and took the pig along, it would be more colourful. Police were ordered to search for these knights, but I don't know if they found anything."

"Whoever it was on that spit," said Toni, "it must be someone really deeply hated. To go to such trouble and risk of being found out! If you hadn't recognised it wasn't a pig, Agatha, there would have been a lot of cannibals at Winter Parva."

"I'm tired," said Roy. "I bet I'm going to have nightmares. I'm off to bed."

"I think I'll go home," said Charles. "Toni can sleep on the sofa."

Toni smiled at him gratefully. She had switched off her mobile phone. She had mixed feelings. She felt she was being disloyal to Paul, and yet detective work was her life, and uneasily she remembered the times when Paul had laughed indulgently about her job.

Agatha's phone rang. She answered it. "Oh, Paul, it's you," Toni heard her say. "No, not here. She said something about going down to Southampton to see her mother. . . . What? . . . Yes, I'll tell her." She rang off. "I didn't think you wanted to see him tonight."

"Not tonight," agreed Toni. "I'll talk to him tomorrow."

■ ■ ■ ■

The next morning, after breakfast, they all waited eagerly for the news on television. The report was disappointingly short. Roy shrieked again with dismay over his appearance. "I'm starting growing my hair today," he said.

There came a ring at the doorbell. When Agatha answered it, she found Inspector Wilkes, Bill Wong, another detective she did not know and a policewoman standing on the doorstep.

"Come in," said Agatha. "Toni, Charles and Roy are all in the living room. Do you want to interview us all together?"

"We'll start with you, Mrs. Raisin," said Wilkes.

"Then come through to the kitchen," said Agatha.

When they were all seated around the kitchen table, Agatha was taken over her statement again. When the questioning was over, she asked eagerly, "What's the latest?"

Bill said, "The butcher who was supposed to deliver the pig to the roast was found drugged and bound up in his shop. We still have not established the identity of the dead man. Now, we would like to speak to your assistant, Toni Gilmour."

By the time the police left, they all felt shaky and very tired. Delayed shock was settling in. Roy said weakly that he would like to go back to bed, and Toni said she would go home. Charles decided to leave as well.

Agatha poured herself a hot-water bottle for comfort and retreated with her cats to her bed. As she drifted off into sleep, she remembered shouting about that awful policeman and wishing he would roast in hell on a spit. Her eyes flew open. Someone or some people had viciously hated whoever it was they had killed. People still shouted the epithet of "pig" at policemen. Too far-fetched, she told herself, go back to sleep. But sleep would not come.

She flicked open the address book she kept beside the bed and found Bill Wong's mobile number.

When he answered, Agatha asked, "Any policemen missing?"

"What do you mean?"

"The dead man," said Agatha. "People call the police pigs. Just a thought."

Bill laughed. "You should write fiction, Agatha. Forget it. Leave it to the police. I don't want you meddling in this one. These killers will be highly dangerous."

38

Feeing rather silly, Agatha said goodbye and fell into a deep sleep.

"What did the Raisin woman want?" asked Wilkes the following morning. He had overheard Bill's end of the conversation during the previous night.

Bill gave a reluctant laugh. "Mrs. Raisin has just suggested that the dead man might be a policeman."

"And where did that flight of fancy come from?"

"Policemen are often called pigs, and so she has leapt to that conclusion."

"Ridiculous. Now, pass me that roster. I want every man out on this case. Get Police Sergeant Tulloch in here."

When Tulloch entered the room, Wilkes said, "Are they all in the briefing room? I'll be along in a few moments."

"All there," said Tulloch, a burly Scot with a shock of fair hair. "Oh, except Beech. I've phoned his home, but there's no reply."

Wilkes and Bill looked at each other in sudden consternation. "You don't think . . . ," began Wilkes.

"He's never missed a day before," said Bill uneasily.

"Get round there," said Wilkes, "and take Detective Peterson with you."

39

Bill brightened. Alice Peterson had recently joined them from Gloucester CID to replace Detective Collins, an acidulous woman, who, to Bill's relief, had finally secured a transfer to London — not to Scotland Yard, her ambition, but to Brixton.

Alice was clever and almost pretty with her neat dark curls and blue eyes.

On the road to Beech's home, Bill told her about Agatha Raisin's odd idea. "I've heard about Mrs. Raisin," said Alice. "She has had a lot of successes in the past. Everyone says she just blunders into things and gets lucky, but I think she must be clever."

"In this case, I hope not. Here we are."

Bill parked in front of a trim little cottage on the outskirts of Winter Parva.

"Why doesn't he live in Mircester?" asked Alice.

"It's cheaper here, he says. Let's go."

There was no doorbell, but there was a large brass doorknocker in the shape of a lion's head. Bill performed an energetic rat-a-tat on it.

Silence.

Both detectives looked at each other. They knew from experience that empty houses have a particular silence.

Bill tried the door. "It's locked," he said,

"and the curtains at the front window are closed. I'll go round the back. You keep an eye on the front."

The previous night's fog had thinned to a mist. Bill went along a path at the side of the house. There was a conservatory at the back of the house. Bill looked in.

It was a mess. Plants had been pulled out of their pots and lay on the floor. Bill called Alice, who came hurrying round to join him.

"We're going to have to break in," said Bill.

"Try the conservatory door first," urged Alice.

Bill turned the handle and the door opened. "We'd better suit up," said Bill. When they were covered in their blue plastic forensic suits, they stepped inside, calling, "Beech!" in loud voices.

They entered the kitchen. Every canister, box of cereal and bag of flour had been emptied onto the floor. They then went to the living room, followed by a search of a small dining room, and then went upstairs to the bedrooms. Chaos was everywhere: drawers pulled out, clothes thrown around, mattresses slit open. Everywhere in the house appeared to have been frantically searched. Floorboards were torn up, curtains pulled down and carpets ripped up.

The sinister silence of the house and the outside village seemed to press on their ears. Bill opened the door to the bathroom and let out an exclamation of dismay.

There was blood everywhere. It was spattered up the walls and all over the bath.

They retreated outside and sat in their car with the engine running to keep warm. "Agatha was right," said Bill. "How does she do it?"

"I noticed something odd," said Alice.

"What's that?"

"I've a brother in the antiques business. Some of those pieces of furniture in the living room are very valuable. How could a mere constable afford, say, a Georgian bureau?"

"Beats me. I hear sirens. There's nothing we can do now until the Scenes of Crimes Operatives are finished. I hope they find the head."

"What?"

"Gary Beech's head. I wonder what happened to that?"

Agatha and Roy went to the pub for dinner that evening. The pub was crowded, but Agatha managed to thrust her way through to the only vacant table, reaching it before a stocky villager, Mrs. Benson, was about to

42

claim it.

"I'll just need to join you," said Mrs. Benson.

"You can't," said Agatha, still too upset by the horror of the murder to be polite. "We want to talk in private."

"Well, I never did!" exclaimed Mrs. Benson.

"Then start," said Agatha, sitting down and turning her back on the woman.

Mrs. Benson glared at her and then left the pub in a huff. She looked at her watch. It was coming up to seven o'clock. If she hurried, she could listen to *The Archers* serial on Radio 4 and make some toasted cheese.

Before *The Archers,* the news came on. She listened as the announcer said that the murdered man was a policeman named Gary Beech. All of a sudden, Mrs. Benson remembered Agatha Raisin shouting threats against Beech in the village shop and saying he should be roasted on a spit. *The Archers* serial forgotten, she phoned police headquarters in Mircester.

The last train to London had left Moreton-in-Marsh, so Agatha drove Roy to Oxford and waved him goodbye.

As she drove back, snow was beginning to

fall. She still felt very tired after a gruelling drive. Her car had skidded several times on the road down into Carsely.

Her heart sank as she saw a police Land Rover parked outside her cottage.

"Now what?" she demanded of the uncaring white wilderness outside.

As she got out of her car, a policeman approached her and said, "You are to come with us to police headquarters."

"Why?" demanded Agatha truculently.

"You'll find out when you get there," said the policeman.

Mircester looked like a Christmas card with the tall towers of its snow-covered and floodlit abbey looming behind police headquarters.

Agatha was told to wait in the reception area. It had recently been redecorated in the hope that it might look more people-friendly, but the plastic palms were dusty and the walls painted sulphurous yellow. Agatha wondered if it had been painted on the cheap, because little patches of the former institutional green were showing through in places.

Detective Alice Peterson appeared and summoned Agatha, who followed her to an interview room. Agatha sat opposite Bill and

Wilkes. Alice put a tape in the recording machine and the interview began.

"We are awaiting DNA results," said Wilkes, "but a search of policeman Gary Beech's house led us to believe he is the victim. Now, you were heard in the village shop in Carsely threatening Gary Beech's life and saying that you hoped he would roast on a spit in hell. What have you to say to that? And despite the thick fog at Winter Parva, you immediately identified the supposed pig as a man."

Agatha briefly remembered when she had first moved to Carsely that it had been more of a close-knit village community. Now newcomers came and went. Who had reported her? Her thoughts flew to Mrs. Ada Benson.

"We're waiting," snapped Wilkes.

"It's like this," said Agatha. "Gary Beech gave me a ticket for blowing my nose while my car was parked in a queue of cars on the Carsely road because of roadworks. He then ticketed me for doing thirty-two miles an hour. I was very angry and let off steam in the shop. I had a guest for the week-end."

"Name?"

"You know who."

"Stop being obstructive and answer the question for the tape."

45

Agatha heaved a weary sigh. "Roy Silver."

"And?"

"And I saw the pig roast advertised amongst local events. My detective, Toni Gilmour, was invited and she came with a friend, Paul Finlay. Charles Fraith opted to join us as well. When we got to the pig roast . . . I've told you all this already."

"Just go over it again."

"When I got to the pig roast, the fog shifted a bit and some of the villagers were holding flaming torches — flambeaux. I saw a tattoo on what I at first took to be the pig's haunch. Then I realised it was a heart with an arrow through it and the name Amy."

"Other people," said Wilkes, "would have assumed someone had been having fun with the pig."

"I shone my torch on the pig's head and saw it had been stitched on. In a flash, I realised it was the body of a naked man," said Agatha defiantly.

"Had you ever come across Gary Beech before he charged you in those two incidents?"

"No."

"And yet you suggested to Detective Sergeant Wong here that the body might be

46

that of Gary Beech? That seems very suspicious."

"Oh, for goodness' sakes," howled Agatha, "I didn't mention his name. I suggested the victim might be a policeman. If I had anything to do with the pillock's murder, would I have made such a suggestion?"

"You may have done." And so the questioning went on and on until Agatha, warned not to leave the country, and with her eyes gritty with fatigue, was allowed to leave.

Alice ran her home. "I'll be glad to get some sleep," she said. "And I hope I don't get nightmares."

"What was at his house?" asked Agatha.

Alice was sure Wilkes would be furious with her for discussing the murder, but Agatha was a friend of Bill's and she liked Bill.

"Blood everywhere in the bathroom, in the bath and up the walls. Why did you really think the dead man might be him?"

"I didn't. But he must have infuriated an awful lot of people apart from me," said Agatha. "You see, I rely a lot on intuition, as I don't have the resources of the police. Was he married?"

"Divorced. The ex-wife is on holiday in Florida."

"Really? Does she have a lot of money of her own?"

"Not unless she met a rich man we don't know about. Before her marriage, she worked as a checkout girl at a supermarket. But Gary must have had some money because I spotted some good antiques in his living room. The place had been ransacked."

When they arrived at Agatha's cottage, Alice said hurriedly, "Please don't tell anyone I discussed the case with you. I could get into the most awful trouble."

"Not a word," promised Agatha. "Thank goodness the snow's stopped and they've gritted the road."

Agatha tried to find out more about Gary Beech but was held back by having to attend to the cases where she was being paid for her detective work.

Some of the work involved a lot of standing around in the cold and watching houses for signs of erring spouses. Agatha hated divorce cases, but the country was in a deep recession and she just had to be grateful for any work.

The weather continued to be bitterly cold. People were beginning to wonder if all this global warming was some trick of the nanny state to bully them into fines for not separating their garbage, for having to employ a chimney sweep every three months, and wondering how soon it would be before spy planes flew over their houses to check their carbon footprints.

The villagers of Carsely, united in misery, had marched on the Town Hall in Mircester to protest against the frequent power cuts.

Agatha decided to buy a generator, thinking it would be simple to install. The contractor was a lugubrious man who seemed to see fire and disaster all about.

Agatha's suggestion that he put the generator in the kitchen caused him to raise his red mottled hands in horror. "Can't do that, love," he said. "The gases that come out o' that there petrol machine are lethal. Needs to be outside the house. But 'er can't be getting wet. You'll need a liddle hut for 'er."

But at last a carpenter had finished building a little shed outside the kitchen door and the contractor had departed, after leaving Agatha with a handbook in six languages, the size of a Bible.

Returning home after a cold day's work two weeks after the murder of Gary Beech, Agatha found the electricity was off again. She carefully followed the instructions, the generator roared into life and the electricity came on.

She was relaxing in front of the television set with a large gin and tonic in one hand and a cigarette in the other when her doorbell rang.

When Agatha opened the door, she found the vicar's wife there, and behind her, two elderly couples.

"May we come in, Mrs. Raisin?"

"Of course," said Agatha. "What's up?"

"This is Mr. and Mrs. Friend and Mr. and Mrs. Terence. They do not have money for fuel, and they are too old to cope with this biting cold. Could you possibly give them shelter until the power comes on?"

Agatha wanted to scream, "No!" But the calm eyes of the vicar's wife were fastened on her face.

"All right," she said reluctantly.

"I'll phone you as soon as the power comes on," said Mrs. Bloxby, "and then I'll come and pick them up."

When she had left, Agatha helped the elderly people out of their coats and wraps and settled them in the living room. She asked them if they had eaten, and they said yes, they had. She then asked them if they would like something to drink, and they all murmured in agreement. Being old, they all needed frequent trips upstairs to the bathroom. The Terences were all right, but the

Friends needed assistance up the stairs. To exhausted Agatha, it seemed as if she had just got one of them settled when the other would pipe up that he or she had to go to the "you-know-what."

And as the hours passed, the generator continued to chug away. Agatha kept opening the front door and gazing anxiously down the street to see if the lights had come on again in the village. The contractor had warned her that the wiring could not take the load of both generator and restored power or "the house will burn to ashes."

Mrs. Bloxby phoned. "This is terrible," she said. "I keep phoning the electricity company and they say, 'Power will be restored momentarily,' but nothing happens. How are they?"

Agatha walked with her new cordless telephone to the living room door. "They've all fallen asleep. Look, I'll give it a little longer." As she replaced the receiver, the lights came on. She rushed to switch off the generator.

Mrs. Bloxby phoned back. "I'm on my way."

Agatha woke her sleeping guests. Mr. Friend struggled to his feet. "I hope you never find who murdered that copper," he said.

"Why?" asked Agatha.

"He was going to get me up in the court and do me for flashing."

"What! How did that happen?"

"I was out for a walk with the missus, and I had to pee. Went behind a bush. No one about, or so I thought. That damn Beech, he came out of nowhere and charged me with exposing myself. Me! I've been a churchgoer all me life. The shame of it. I could ha' murdered the man meself."

"Did you go to court?" asked Agatha.

"No, but it got in the local paper, and mud sticks. I'm telling you, missus, I don't know how the police are going to find the murderer because there's so many wanted him dead."

CHAPTER THREE

Agatha overslept. As soon as she poked her nose over the duvet, she felt the room was cold. She switched on the bedside lamp and nothing happened.

She struggled out of bed and picked out her warmest clothes. Clumping downstairs later in a pair of fleece-lined suede boots, she wondered if she would ever wear high heels again. Nothing more depressing than flat-heeled footwear.

She did not want to switch on the generator, for the thought of operating the machine gave her a stab of techno fear.

Agatha phoned the electricity company and gave them a blast of abuse that didn't bring the power on but made her feel much better.

The radio in the car informed her that salt was being imported from abroad. Agatha wondered how they could spare it, as the European continent was pretty much snowed up.

Her office was in an old building in a narrow winding street near the abbey. She pounded up the stairs to the first floor and swung open the frosted glass door of the office.

Toni, Patrick Mulligan and Phil Marshall were all talking excitedly as Agatha came in.

"What's up?" demanded Agatha, taking off her coat.

"We've got a client," said Toni, "and you'll never guess who it is"

"Enlighten me," said Agatha crossly, irritated with herself for being late.

"Gary Beech's ex-wife," said Toni. "She's employing us to find out who murdered her ex-husband."

"And you didn't even phone me? You let her get out of the office before I arrived?"

Phil smoothed his silver hair and said quietly, "She's waiting for you at her home address. We thought we'd wait until you arrived."

"And why aren't you all out working?"

"It's such good news," said Patrick, looking more like a tired bloodhound than ever. "Toni wanted us all to wait until we told you. Gary's wife is now a Mrs. Richards, married to a supermarket owner. She's prepared to pay a lot."

54

Agatha felt mean and petty. "I'm sorry," she said. "It was good of all of you to wait for me. Do you know why she wants to find the murderer of her ex? If she divorced him, she can't care that much about who killed him."

"Get this," said Toni excitedly. "*He* divorced her!"

"Give me the address and I'll get round there," said Agatha, putting on her coat.

Mrs. Richards lived in a large villa in the better part of town. Snow began to fall again in feathery flakes, swirling hypnotically in front of Agatha's eyes as she drove up the short drive and parked her car.

I should have asked how much she's paying, thought Agatha. She rang the bell and listened to the dulcet tones of the Westminster chimes.

The door opened. Agatha blinked. "Is Mrs. Richards at home?"

"I'm Mrs. Richards. You can call me Amy. You're Agatha Raisin?"

"That's right."

"Come in."

Amy Richards was a petite blonde with a genuine tan and a perfect figure. She had a heart-shaped face and wide blue eyes. When she let Agatha into a living room on the ground floor and the white light from the snow outside fell on Amy's face, Agatha realised that she was older than she looked and that she'd probably had a face-lift. It was because of Amy's eyes. Clever plastic surgery can restore an appearance of youth, but nothing changes the expression of age and experience in the eyes. She was wearing a blue cashmere sweater, the exact colour of her eyes — no, not her eyes, thought Agatha, her contact lenses — and form-fitting grey cashmere trousers over ankle boots with high heels.

"Take a pew," said Amy in a soft Gloucestershire accent. "Drinkie?"

"Nothing," said Agatha. She pulled a notebook out of her capacious handbag. "I was amazed to learn that your husband divorced you. Why?"

"I think there was someone else."

Agatha looked at the vision in front of her and then thought of the squat and ugly Beech.

"I find that hard to believe," she said. "I saw your ex when he gave me a ticket. Hardly an Adonis."

"Wait. I want to show you something."

Amy left the room and returned after a few minutes with a photograph, which she handed to Agatha. "That's me and Gary on our wedding day."

The Amy in the photograph was small and plump, with brown hair and teeth that stuck out. "I was hardly a beauty," she said.

"How did the transformation take place? Was it due to your present husband?"

"No, it was like this. Gary was mean. He used to beat me. But I did love him. I've always fallen for masterful men. But he gave me a good lot of money in the divorce settlement. I was that broke up, I went to Florida on a holiday. The airline had made a mistake with my booking, so as a compensation, they upgraded me to first class. I met this businessman, Art, ever so kind he was. His wife had just dumped him. He was going to finalise the divorce when he got to Miami. I told him all about Gary and he said, 'Get a makeover and let him see what he's been missing.' I said that surely it cost a lot of money.

"He said he would fund it, but I had to meet up with him afterwards and go with him to meet his ex-wife because he wanted to make her jealous."

"What was his full name?"

"Art Mackenzie the third. He said he was in hedge funds. I thought he meant he was a gardener. He tried to explain, but I couldn't understand it."

"What puzzles me is why he just didn't buy the services of some beauty in Florida."

"He said I reminded him of his mother."

Stark, raving bonkers, thought Agatha. But she prompted, "Go on."

"Well, it took over three months and I had the works. He must have spent a fortune on me. When I was finished, he said he was delighted, so I said, 'When do we meet your wife?' He said, not yet. But he said I should do some work for him. He said he ran a big escort agency and some Arabs were coming to town. He said all I had to do was act pretty and see they had plenty of drinks in their penthouse suite. He had changed. Before I started all the cosmetic surgery and that, he cried a lot and said I was a comfort to him. But afterwards, he had gone sort of hard and businesslike and kept rabbiting on about how much I had cost him.

"Well, I was pretty green but not that green, and I knew he wanted me to do some whoring for him. I felt sick. I was sitting in this hotel lounge, crying, because I had no money to get a plane home."

"You could have gone to the British consul," said Agatha.

Her eyes widened. "I never thought of that. I'd never been out of England before. But that was when I met Bunchie."

58

"Who's Bunchie?"

"Mr. Richards. His name is really Tom, but I call him Bunchie. It's a pet name. Anyway, he came up to me and asked what was the matter, and the minute I heard his English voice, I cried even harder. He said I should go to the police, but I said they'd think I was nothing more than a tart for taking his money in the first place and they might arrest me for prostitution. So he said he had to catch the plane home, and do you know, when he said he lived in Mircester, I thought, There really is a God, cos I'd been praying ever so hard. And he said he'd take me with him. We got married two weeks after we got back."

"Have you considered," said Agatha, "that this Art may have come to England looking for you and taken his spite out on Gary?"

She bit her collagen-enhanced lips. "I dunno."

"What does your husband think about paying my agency to find out what happened to Beech? I mean, it's nothing to do with him."

"Oh, he'd do anything for me. He's got oodles of money and gives me a very generous allowance, which is just as well, because I suppose I'll have to pay to send you to Florida."

"Let's get back to your marriage to Gary. How did you meet?"

"He came into the supermarket regular like, to buy his beer. Then he asked me out. He took me to all the best places. Fair bowled off my feet, I was."

"Did you never worry where he got the money from? Surely you must have known that a copper's pay doesn't amount to all that much?"

"I asked once and he took his belt to me and told me not to ask questions again."

"My dear girl, why didn't you leave him?"

"Well, Dad used to beat me something awful. I thought it was something that men did. Then Gary started to stay out all night, and I thought there was someone else. One night when he was asleep, I got the key to his desk and began to search it, looking for love letters. He caught me. Broke my ribs, he did. Then he said he was getting rid of me and he'd be generous if I just got the hell out."

"Let me see if I have this right. This man beat you, abused you, divorced you, and you still want to find out what happened to him?"

"I have to know. I think it was something to do with that other woman."

"But you have no proof there was another

woman."

"Well, several times when the phone rang and I answered it, whoever it was just hung up."

"Have you told the police about the man in Florida?"

"I didn't like to. Didn't want to sound like a tart."

Agatha thought quickly. She really ought to urge her to go to the police. The FBI in Florida would surely ferret out this Art Mackenzie, if that really was his name. Was Amy as naïve as she seemed?

"I want this Art made to suffer," said Amy. "Have you ever had cosmetic surgery? Silly me. Of course you haven't. Well, it's damn painful, and what with getting my teeth straightened and the liposuction and all that, I'd like to get a bit of my own back."

"I still wonder why he picked you," said Agatha. "He could have found plenty of pretty girls in Florida without having to go to all the expense of making them over."

"I do think he loved me for a bit," said Amy. "And do you know, when he showed me a picture of his mother, I did look a bit like her."

"Well," said Agatha, looking out of the window at the freezing day outside, "I may as well start with Florida. You will be billed for all expenses plus a daily fee."

"Oh, yes, your Mrs. Freedman told me that and got me to sign the papers."

"Don't you think it might be a good idea if I talked to your husband as well?"

"He's awfully busy."

"What does he do?"

"He owns Richards Supermarkets."

Agatha recognised the name. The supermarkets were all over the country.

"Let me think this over," said Agatha. "I'll get in touch with you soon."

Agatha called a meeting of her staff early that evening and told them what she had learned from the former Mrs. Beech.

"Lucky you," said Toni. "I wouldn't mind going to Florida."

"I may as well see if there's any connection between this Art person and Beech. There's not much can be done here at the moment that the police can't. Did Amy say anything about telling the police about the prostitution racket?"

"No, not a thing," said Patrick. "She said she'd been on holiday in Florida and that's where she met her new husband. I never heard that she'd mentioned this fellow Art."

"It all seems a bit coincidental," said Toni. "I mean, how fortunate this Richards turned up at the right moment to rescue her and comes from Mircester as well."

"What if the whole thing is a pack of lies?" said Phil. "I mean, you do have a reputation, Agatha."

"Reputation for what?" demanded Agatha furiously.

"For being a good detective," said Phil. "She's no doubt read in the papers or heard from the police about you finding the body. So the best way to keep you close is to hire you. Even better, if she simply used the divorce money to go to Florida for plastic surgery, it's a good excuse to get out of the country and off the case."

"And," put in Patrick, "this Richards may be involved in the murder. She was definitely out of the country, but where was he? I think you should wait here for a bit, Agatha."

The wind howled round the old building, and sleet pattered against the windows.

"I'm going," said Agatha. "I'll visit her again this evening and see if I can catch her with Bunchie."

"Who's Bunchie?" asked Toni.

"It's her pet name for him. Talking about pets, how's Paul?"

"Very well, thank you," said Toni primly.

"Seeing a lot of him?"

"Has this anything to do with the agency?" asked Toni angrily.

"Well, no, but —"

"So mind your own business."

"May I remind you, Mizz Gilmour, that you are speaking to your employer?"

"But not my mother." Toni slammed out of the office.

"You asked for that," said Phil. "Leave the girl alone or she might marry Paul to spite you."

Agatha sat alone in the office after the others had left, wondering whether it was really worthwhile going to Florida or had Amy been spinning some tale. Forget Florida, she suddenly thought. Perhaps it was a ruse to get her out of the country. Surely the answer to Beech's death lay in the Cotswolds. Uneasy thoughts about young Simon Black also troubled her mind. What if he was killed in Afghanistan? The names of the dead were now well publicised. Had Toni been falling in love with him? Why on earth had she interfered? A nasty little conscience was reminding her that Toni was not her daughter, and even if she were, she should stop interfering in the girl's life.

She gave herself a shake. Let the police handle the Florida end. She put on her coat and went out into the biting cold and made her way to police headquarters, where she informed the desk that she had important news for Inspector Wilkes.

She was eventually ushered through into an interview room. "What is it now?" asked Wilkes wearily.

Agatha told him everything she had learned from Amy Richards, consulting a sheaf of notes from time to time.

When she had finished, Wilkes surveyed her cynically. "I would have thought, from past experience, that you would have kept this information to yourself, particularly as the woman has engaged your services."

"I cannot quite believe the Florida story, or about the fortuitous meeting with Richards. I think, for some reason, she wants me out of the way."

"You being the great detective, who if left here would solve a case the police can't?"

"Something like that," mumbled Agatha.

"Well, at least you are showing some sense at last. Wait there."

So Agatha waited, longing for a cigarette, tracing patterns on the scarred table in front of her with one fingernail.

At last Wilkes came back with Detective Constable Alice Peterson. He switched on a tape recorder and took Agatha all through her story again. When she had finished, he asked, "Did Mrs. Richards ask you not to tell the police any of this?"

"Not exactly. I know she didn't want me to tell you in case you thought she was some sort of tart. Please, for my sake, go easy on her. I need this contract."

"It's not as if we owe you any favours," said Wilkes.

"You do," said Agatha. "Think of all the times I've helped you out."

Wilkes sighed. "We'll be as tactful as possible. We will say we've traced her recent movements courtesy of the FBI and take it from there."

And with that, Agatha had to be content.

CHAPTER FOUR

Agatha arrived back at her cottage to find Bill Wong waiting for her. "I've been hanging around for ages," complained Bill, seated in the kitchen with one cat round his neck and another on his lap. Agatha was glad to find the heat was back on.

After explaining that she had been at police headquarters and why, Agatha asked, "Why are you here? Any more questions?"

"No, I haven't heard about your latest, but I have heard about Paul Finlay."

"What?"

"He was married until two years ago. His wife divorced him on grounds of cruelty. She got custody of their two children."

"Was it mental cruelty, or physical cruelty?"

"Both."

Agatha covered her face with her hands. "I'm in bad trouble."

"You're in bad trouble? What about Toni?

We've got to warn her."

"Yes, yes. It's not only that. I've done a bad thing."

"Again?"

"It's not funny. Young Simon Black who worked for me was keen on Toni. She's too young to get married, Bill!"

"And you didn't want to lose a good detective," said Bill cynically.

"I told Simon to wait three years and then I wouldn't stand in his way. He joined the army and he's now in Afghanistan."

"Agatha, are you sure your jealousy of Toni doesn't make you think up these horrible plots?"

"No, no. I care for the girl. There was something unstable about Simon."

"Then let's hope anyway he doesn't die a hero. Tell me the latest."

Agatha glanced at her watch. "I hope to visit Amy this evening. I'd better go. I want her to think I'm off to Florida and then I'll go underground."

"She'll see you around."

"I'll disguise myself. But I must get a look at this husband of hers. What are we going to do about Toni?"

"I'll go right now and see her. I've got the evening off."

"Don't tell her about Simon!"

"No, I think that's up to you."

Paul Finlay mounted the narrow stairs to Toni's flat with a feeling of excitement. He felt the fact she had asked him for dinner and had said she had something important to tell him was propitious in the least. Toni was all he desired: young, pretty and surely malleable. A woman's duty was to support her husband at all times and agree with him.

He had never been in Toni's flat before and expected dolls on the sofa and posters of pop groups on the walls. But although it was small, it was furnished in excellent taste. Bookshelves on one wall were full of paperbacks and hardbacks. Two framed prints decorated the opposite wall, a Paul Klee and a Cotswold landscape by an artist he did not recognise. A round table was set at the window.

"Hello, Paul," said Toni nervously. "Want a drink before dinner?"

"What have you got?"

"Beer or wine."

"Wine will be fine. What's that?" He took the bottle from her. "My dear innocent — Blockley Merlot!" Blockley was a village near Moreton-in-Marsh.

"It's a local company who imports it and bottles it. Have you been to the village store in Blockley? It's fabulous, all the things they have there. Charles says this wine is very good."

"I'll stick to beer," said Paul ungraciously.

Toni shrugged. She opened a bottle of beer and poured him a glass. She was wearing cut-off jeans and a faded T-shirt.

"I thought this was to be an occasion," said Paul, surveying her clothes.

"Rather a sad one," said Toni. "Do sit down."

He sat down on a two-seater sofa and patted the space beside him, but Toni drew up a hard chair and sat opposite. Toni had been out on only two dates with him since the murder. On each occasion, he had lectured her on the dangers of her job when he was not pontificating about the importance of his own. Toni wondered what she had ever seen in him. Maybe a psychiatrist would say she had been looking for a substitute father.

"It's like this, Paul," she said. "I am devoted to my job and I haven't got time to go out on dates."

His face became distorted with fury. "Are you *dumping* me?"

"That's a pretty harsh way of putting it," said Toni. "All I'm trying to say — well . . . it's just that we're not suited."

"Little girls like you need a good slap on

70

the bottom." Before Toni quite realised what was happening, he had jerked her off her chair, over his knee, and had begun to spank her. She reached down between their bodies and grabbed his balls and squeezed as hard as she could. He screamed and threw her off and then rolled onto the floor.

At that very opportune moment, the door opened and Bill Wong walked in.

He helped Toni to her feet. "What happened? Did he assault you?"

"He smacked my bottom because I said I didn't want to see him anymore."

Bill hauled the still squirming Paul to his feet and clipped handcuffs on him. He read him his rights and charged him with assault.

"*She* attacked *me!*" Paul howled.

"Let's just forget it," said Toni.

Bill looked at her. "He's done it before and he will do it again. His ex-wife divorced him because of physical and mental cruelty. He broke her ribs on one occasion and her jaw on another. You know the score, Toni."

"Okay," said Toni. "Just take him away."

"Are you going to be all right? Is there anyone you could phone?"

"No, I'll be all right now," said Toni.

Agatha at that moment was telling Amy that she was going to Florida. "Isn't your husband at home?" she asked.

"He should be here at any moment," said Amy nervously.

"You seem on edge," said Agatha.

"I keep wondering if whoever killed poor Gary might come after me."

"Only if they think you know something."

The doorbell rang. "That'll be my Bunchie!" cried Amy, leaping to her feet.

"Doesn't he have a key . . . ?" began Agatha. But the door to the living room opened and Amy entered, followed by a small, square man. He was expensively dressed in grey worsted. He had oily brown hair, a florid face and a long clown's mouth.

"This is my Bunchie!" cried Amy. "Good luck on your trip. Keep in touch."

"If I could just have a few words with your husband, please."

"Oh, now is not the time. My poor Bunchie is so tired."

Somehow Agatha found herself propelled towards the door.

"It's all very odd," Agatha told the privet hedge outside. She settled into her car and drove off a little way down the street where she could still get a good view of the entrance to the house from the streetlamp outside. The cold was intense, but she did not feel like switching on the engine. I

72

wonder if this Bunchie really is her husband, she thought. He didn't have a door key.

After an hour, the door opened and Bunchie appeared. He scuttled into a black BMW and set off. Agatha followed him. He drove through Mircester and out to the northern end of the town where there were large villas set back from the road.

Agatha got out of her car and walked slowly along. He walked up the path of one of the villas, took out keys and unlocked the door. A child's voice could be heard crying shrilly, "Mummy, Daddy's home!"

Now, thought Agatha, retreating to her car, either Amy is on the game or dear Bunchie is a bigamist. If I tell Bill, he'll put a watch on the house and then call her in for questioning. Amy's paying me and I need the money. Expose Amy and I won't get any. But if I continue to watch Amy, there might be some connection there to her ex-husband's murder.

Her plans for choosing some disguise to pretend she had actually gone to Florida while keeping a watch on Amy's house were nearly sabotaged by a letter arriving in the morning post that declared she had been appointed as one of the nominees for the award of Mircester's Woman of the Year.

Agatha glowed. She must slim. She must book a series of nonsurgical face-lifts. But after looking more closely at the invitation, she realised it was not due to take place until June. And usually the nominees for Woman of the Year were announced the year before. The choice of her name looked a bit last minute. She must find out the names of the other nominees.

But in the meantime, it was back to business.

Heavily disguised, Agatha drove into Mircester and checked the voters' roll for the address where she had followed the man who had left Amy's. To her amazement, opposite the address was the name Mr. T. Richards. So it looked as if he was a bigamist! But she could not confront him. She had phoned Amy earlier and had told her that she was about to board a flight to Miami.

Agatha called Bill on his mobile. A sleepy voice answered her and said crossly, "You woke me up."

Agatha looked at her watch. "It's ten o'clock in the morning."

"And I've been working all night," said Bill. "What is it?"

"Can I come round and see you? I have

some important news."

"Okay."

"I'm in diguise."

Fifteen minutes later, Mrs. Wong opened the door to a woman with heavy black hair and plump cheeks, wrapped in several layers of clothing and wearing large glasses.

"We're not buying," she said. The door began to close.

Bill appeared behind his mother, wearing pyjamas and a dressing gown. "It's all right, Mum," he said. "I know who this is. It is you, isn't it?"

"Yes."

"Come on in."

Mrs. Wong retreated, angrily muttering about folks who wouldn't let her boy sleep.

Bill led the way into the living room. "It's a good disguise, Agatha. Out with it. I'm so tired, your information better be good."

Agatha told him what she had found out about Richards.

Bill listened in amazement. "How did he think he would get away with it in the middle of a murder inquiry? Good work. We'll pull him in."

"And you'll keep me up-to-date on anything you find out?" asked Agatha anxiously.

"You have my word. Did Toni tell you I arrested Paul Finlay?"

"No, she never said a word. What happened?"

Bill told her.

"Why on earth didn't Toni tell me?" wondered Agatha.

"Perhaps she feels you are too interested in her private life, Agatha."

Agatha thought dismally of Simon in Afghanistan and blushed. Bill surveyed her in amazement. He could not remember ever having seen Agatha blush before.

By the end of another week, Agatha was tired of her surveillance of both Richards and Amy and driving in disguise to wait for long hours at a time outside their respective houses. Tom Richards spent most of his evenings and nights with Amy and only about two with his children.

It was therefore with relief that she hailed Bill Wong, who was waiting for her at the end of what seemed to Agatha like a very long week of waiting.

"Come in," said Agatha, "and tell me, please, that I can get rid of this disguise. The wig's so heavy, and these pads in my cheeks make me feel like a chipmunk."

"They also make you sound drunk," said Bill, following her into the kitchen. "Make me a cup of coffee and I'll tell you all about it."

Agatha plugged in the percolator after tearing off her wig and clawing the pads out of her cheeks. "I can't wait," she said over her shoulder. "Start talking."

"Tom Richards was divorced amicably from his wife a year ago. He married Amy six months later. She begged for a make-over, face-lift, the works, so he sent her to Los Angeles. She was never in Florida. Asked why she had made up this fairy tale about this Art Mackenzie, it turns out she's a bit of a fantasist, and it was all in a plot she had seen in some soap opera over there. Asked why she had lied, she said that if she had said that she had asked poor Bunchie to pay up so much money for her cosmetic surgery, it would make her look grasping and vain. Thanks."

He took a mug of coffee from Agatha. "Richards supports her story, and yes, he did pay for everything."

Agatha sat down beside him and nursed a cup of coffee. One cat, Hodge, climbed on Bill's lap, and the other, Boswell, tried to lie across his head. He gently lifted both of them onto the floor.

"Something's wrong here," said Agatha. "You didn't tell her that I had spilled the beans?"

"No, we told her we had been checking up on her marital status, that the FBI in Florida had no records of an Art Mackenzie, and she came out with the truth."

"There's something wrong here." Agatha lit a cigarette. "It's like this. The one thing I believe that Amy told me is that Beech abused her. She said her father had beaten her. She said she liked masterful men. I wonder if the face-lift was really her idea, or was Richards being controlling and manipulating. I wonder whether he tried to get his ex to get a face-lift. Then the money from the divorce from Beech. She said he paid her a generous amount. I wonder if he paid her in cash. I'd like to speak to the former Mrs. Richards."

"It's a bit far-fetched, Agatha. I mean, he may not look like much, but he's very, very rich. Rich men can usually get themselves arm candy easily enough."

"Pig! Pig!" said Agatha.

"Are you insulting . . . ?"

"No, no. The pig whatsit."

"Oh, Pygmalion."

"That's the chap."

"No, you're getting a bit carried away. He seems to dote on her."

"But she showed me a photo of herself before the face-lift. She wasn't even pretty."

"I'd backpedal for a bit," said Bill. "Don't want you blundering around in the middle of a police investigation."

Agatha bristled. "She's paying me to find out who killed Gary, and I need the money. That's a point. Money. Beech evidently paid her generously to give him a divorce. Now where does a mere plod get the money to be generous to anyone?"

"We're looking into that. His bank balance only contained a few hundred pounds, but Detective Constable Alice Peterson pointed out when we visited Gary's home that it held some expensive antiques. We traced the antiques dealer. Yes, Gary bought several expensive pieces of furniture and paid cash. So he was up to something on the side."

"Maybe he targeted people the whole time and charged them with this and that and then took bribes."

"No, I don't think so. He delighted in getting people into court."

Bill had just left when Toni arrived. "I want a word with you, Mrs. Raisin," she said.

"Come in," said Agatha. "What's up?"

Toni marched straight through to the kitchen and slammed a wedding invitation down on the table. "This is what's up, you interfering old bag."

Agatha read the invitation. Lance Corporal Simon Black was to wed Sergeant Susan Crispin in Mircester Abbey on June the tenth.

"So?" demanded Agatha. "What the hell has this to do with me?"

"This letter that came with the invitation." Toni handed her an airmail.

Agatha read: "Dear Toni, I would like you to come to my wedding because I have fond times of the work we did together. I would have married you then, but Agatha told me you were too young and to go away and think about it for three years. I couldn't bear to go on snubbing you and seeing you hurt. So I joined the army. Luckily I met Susie, who's the girl for me, so maybe Agatha was right all along not to trust me. Love, Simon."

"Thanks to your interference, he could be blown up out there," said Toni. "I am eighteen years old, not a child. Do not interfere in my life again. Oh, and take a month's notice."

Agatha sank down into a chair as Toni stormed out.

"Anyone home?" came Charles's voice.

"Oh, do walk in and stamp all over my

feelings," howled Agatha, and burst into tears.

Charles waited until Agatha had finished crying and said gently, "I saw Toni driving off like a bat out of hell. Has she found out about Simon?"

Agatha sniffed miserably. "She forgot these." She pushed the wedding invitation and the letter in front of him.

Charles read both carefully. "I see."

"And she's given a month's notice."

"You shouldn't have interfered."

"I know, I know. It wasn't *all* selfish. It wasn't all because I didn't want to lose a good detective. But there was something unstable about Simon. I sensed it."

"You should have let her find out for herself."

"What about Paul Finlay? If I hadn't found out from Bill he was a wife beater and if Bill hadn't gone round to her flat, she would not have been rescued from a beating."

"Didn't she try to defend herself?"

"Well, yes," admitted Agatha. "She grabbed him by the balls."

"Toni can fight her own battles. She's been taking classes in judo. I think maybe Bill arrived in the nick of time to rescue Paul."

81

"What about the time that creep took her to Paris and she begged me for help? Who got her out of that mess? Me! That's who. She's just going to lurch from one hopeless man to another."

"Like you, Aggie."

"What on earth do you mean?"

"Your first husband was a drunk, your second husband is a coldhearted confirmed bachelor type, and you nearly married a control freak and *I* had to come and rescue *you*."

"That's different."

"It's not. Oh, let's not quarrel. How are you going to get Toni to stay?"

"Try giving her the top jobs and nothing else. Keep out of her way."

The next day in the office, Agatha greeted her staff breezily as if nothing had happened. "Toni," she said, "I want you to give whatever jobs you have to Patrick and Phil. I've got a big one for you. Let me outline the case to date."

They all listened intently. When Agatha had finished, she said, "Toni, I want you to go and see the first Mrs. Richards. Try to find out if Richards wanted her to have a face-lift. I'm working on the theory that he might be a nasty, manipulative man."

"Give me the address," said Toni.

Agatha handed it to her. "I'm going to type out what I've just told all of you so it can be checked on the computer at any time. Patrick, if you have any spare time today, I want you to get on to your old police contacts and find out if they have any suggestions how Beech could have been making money on the side."

Toni gathered up her belongings and left the office. Agatha looked wistful as she watched her go.

Toni felt emotionally numb as she drove in the direction of the Richardses' villa. She pushed out of her mind all the times Agatha had come to her rescue, beginning with saving her from her alcoholic brother and finding her a flat and a job.

The Richardses' home was an imposing villa screened from the road by a thick thorn hedge and a stone wall. She opened the gate and walked up a short gravel drive to the front door.

A woman answered the door, a fairly elderly woman wearing an old-fashioned floral apron. "Mrs. Richards?"

"No, I'm just the cleaner. Her's out."

"Do you know when she'll be back?"

"Around the time the children get out o'

school."

"Is there anywhere in Mircester I might find her?"

"Her might be at that new health bar for lunch. Rubbish, I calls it. Pay a fortune for a bit o' lettuce."

Toni thanked her and left. She knew where the health bar was. A chill wind was blowing from the northeast, and lowering clouds threatened snow. What a day for rabbit food, thought Toni. More like a day for soup and steak and kidney pie. Her stomach rumbled. She had been so upset over Simon's wedding that she only had a cup of coffee for breakfast.

She parked in the main square and, bending her head before the rising wind, picked her way gingerly through the rapidly freezing slush to Barry Wynd, where she knew the health bar was located. She cursed the weather, which seemed to be involved in a vicious cycle of thaw and freeze.

The bar was called Green Happiness. The windows were steamed up, so Toni could not see who was inside. She pushed open the door and went in. There were very few customers. The people of Mircester preferred cholesterol and loads of it.

A sullen waitress with a bad case of acne approached Toni after she had taken a table in the corner, facing the door. Toni looked at the menu and ordered vegetable soup, to be followed by cauliflower and cheese and a glass of an elderberry drink.

To her relief, the soup was accompanied by bread rolls and butter. She looked around. Two women, quite elderly, were sitting by the window. The only other customer apart from Toni herself was a severe-looking man with glasses and a long beard.

The door opened just as Toni was finishing her meal with a cup of dandelion coffee. The woman who entered was tall and dressed in pseudocountry wear: a Barbour worn over a cashmere sweater and cord knee breeches, thick woollen stockings and stout brogues. She had a long, mild face that reminded Toni of a sheep. The rings on her fingers were many and sparkled in the light.

When she called over the waitress and gave her order, her voice was revealed as coming from someone who was trying desperately to sound posh, and failing. The other customers had left. Now there was only Toni and what she hoped was Mrs. Richards.

She smiled vaguely in Toni's direction. Toni boldly rose and went to join her.

"I thought I recognised you," said Toni.

85

"Are you Mrs. Richards?"

"I was. If you're from the press, you want the present wife."

A small dessert bowl of a salad consisting mostly of bean sprouts was placed in front of Mrs. Richards.

"I'm not from the press," said Toni. "Excuse me, but on this freezing day, is that all you're going to eat?"

"Yes. My ex-husband says I have to watch my figure."

"What's it got to do with him?" asked Toni. "He's your ex."

"He's the father of our children, and I rely on him for maintenance. Now, go away."

"I am a detective," said Toni, passing over her card. "Now, our agency is supposed to be working for the present Mrs. Richards, but I feel there is something very odd about her."

"Nothing odder than common little slut."

"Why don't we discuss this over lunch?"

"I'm having lunch."

"No, you are not. You are punishing yourself. You are slim enough. Leave the rabbit food alone and come with me to the nearest pub and we'll have steak and kidney pie and a good bottle of wine."

Mrs. Richards poked dismally at her salad. "What if he finds out?"

"I won't tell him, you won't tell him. Look, I think you've been through a lot," said Toni, "and that no one ever listens to you. But I'm here. Come on. Live a little."

Over steak and kidney pies and a good bottle of Merlot, Mrs. Richards thawed, unlike the weather outside. As Mrs. Richards ate hungrily, Toni talked generally about the weather and told several funny stories of trying to recover lost animals. "I was asked to help find a lost cat called Napoleon. I at last found the animal actually up in the branches of a tall horse chestnut tree in the woman's garden. I climbed up. It was difficult because the wind was blowing strongly and the cat was almost at the top. Just as I was reaching out for it, the wretched animal promptly nipped down to the ground, branch by branch. I followed and chased that cat and finally caught it by taking it in a rugby tackle."

Ms. Richards giggled, a surprisingly girlish giggle. "You can't rugby tackle a cat."

"Oh, yes, you can," said Toni. "What about a brandy with the coffee?"

"Oh, maybe I shouldn't . . ."

Toni raised her voice and called for two brandies.

"Did you know the present Mrs. Amy

Richards?"

"Oh, yes. Look, call me Fiona. We worked in the same supermarket. She was on the till and I stacked the shelves."

"Seems a rather menial job for you. What about the care of your children?"

"We had . . . have . . . an excellent nanny for the two youngest: that's Carol, aged four, and Josie, aged five. My eldest, my boy, Wolfgang, is at Mircester High. He's thirteen."

"Wolfgang is an odd name for a British child."

"Tom's father is German. He insisted the boy was named after him. He's called Wolf at school, so he doesn't mind. My husband thought I should understand the workings of his business empire from the ground up. I didn't mind the shelf stacking. It was a peaceful, mindless job. I got to know Amy. The others knew I was the boss's wife and thought I had been put there to spy on them, but Amy would chatter away to me.

"I invited her back one afternoon for tea. We both had the same day off. I thought Tom was away on business, but he turned up. He started questioning Amy about how much she thought was being sold and what were the most popular items. Soon they were deep in conversation and seemed to have forgotten I existed.

"A few weeks later, Tom asked me for a divorce. At first I was shattered, but when he explained he would pay maintenance, the thought that I could jack in my job and stay at home with the children suddenly seemed like a road out of hell. Goodness, what a listener you are. I shouldn't be criticising Tom."

"I just wondered," said Toni cautiously, "whether Tom ever suggested improvements to your appearance."

"Night and day," said Fiona Richards gloomily. "He wanted me to go out to L.A. and get a face-lift. He always chose my clothes, but that was one thing too far. I tried to laugh and say I wanted to reach an elegant old age and . . . and . . . he hit me."

"Didn't you go to the police?"

"He would have hired the best lawyers. I felt I wouldn't have a chance. So I bought a tape recorder and I began to record all the vicious rows and the sound of the beatings. My small salary was paid into an account in my name. I went to that bank and hired a safe deposit box and put copies of all the tapes into it. Then I told him I was going to the police with the evidence.

"He stormed out of the house, but when he came back, he said that he had fallen in love with Amy and would give me a divorce. I couldn't believe my luck until he finally moved out. He comes back regularly to see the children. Oh, he's all right with them. I bumped into Amy before she got her cosmetic alterations. She was very friendly, but she said an odd thing just as she was leaving. She said, 'I miss Gary. Gary would have sorted him out.' "

"So it looks as if she was off her new husband before she even went to the States," said Toni.

"Now, how am I to get home? I'm over the limit."

"I'll get you a cab," said Toni. "Is there anyone who can come and get your car?"

"Yes, the nanny, Mrs. Drufus." She leaned forward and looked earnestly at Toni. "Do you think Tom killed Gary?"

"If it had just been a blow on the head, I could believe it," said Toni. "But to kill a man — he was evidently knifed to death — and then to cut off his head and try to get him roasted as a pig — no. It sounds to me like the work of several people."

"Would you keep in touch with me?" asked Fiona plaintively. "You're such a good listener. Now, if I had a daughter like you . . . Oh, well."

She rose somewhat unsteadily to her feet.

Toni found her a taxi and sent her on her way.

Agatha cursed under her breath. The girl's report on Fiona Richards was so good. Toni, with her youth and air of innocence, could winkle stories out of people who would otherwise have clammed up when faced with Agatha herself.

After leaving a note on Toni's desk thanking her for her work, along with Simon's letter and wedding invitation, Agatha went out into the freezing cold. The time had come to ask Amy Richards why she had lied. Agatha realised she would need to tell the truth and confess she had never gone to Florida.

Amy answered the door. She wasn't wearing her contact lenses, showing her eyes were brown. She looked as if she had been crying.

"Oh, it's you," she said bleakly.

Agatha shivered. "Let me in."

She pushed past the slim figure of Amy and into the living room. Agatha removed her heavy coat and a shawl that made her feel she looked like Mother Machree, cursing all antifur activists under her breath. Mink were vermin. They should be clothing her back instead of marauding around the countryside, killing off the native species.

"Amy, I haven't been to Florida." Agatha sat down on a sofa, and Amy sat in an armchair facing her. Between them was a glass coffee table holding glossy magazines — *OK!, Celebrity, Vogue* and colour supplements from various Sunday papers.

"Why?" asked Amy in a croaky voice.

"I'm sorry to say this, Amy, but I did not believe you. A police contact told me that you have confessed that you were lying, that you were never in Florida and it was Tom Richards who paid for you to go to L.A. for the transformation. I naturally began to wonder if you wanted me out of the way and why."

"I told the police the truth this time. I didn't want them to think I was a gold digger. I mean, it takes an awful lot of money to look like this."

Hadn't Dolly Parton once said something like "It takes an awful lot of money to look this cheap," thought Agatha, for there was something rather *tawdry* about Amy that day. She was wearing high-heeled pink shoes, a tight pink sweater and pink pedal pushers.

"So it was not your husband that suggested you have plastic surgery?"

"No, of course not."

"But he suggested it to his previous wife. Is he a bully?"

"Oh, no, my Bunchie's the sweetest, dearest man."

"Okay. Let's get back to Gary. You said he gave you a lot of money for the divorce. A cheque?"

"No, it was cash."

"How much?"

"I c-can't remember."

"Amy!"

"It was about ten thousand in an envelope. He said, 'Take it and come with me to the lawyer's, but don't mention the money. Tell him you don't want anything from me. Get it!' So I went along with it."

"But you surely had a lawyer of your own."

"There was one in the same building."

"Who are these lawyers?"

"Crumley, Fatch and Blinder."

"And where are they?"

"They're out in the industrial estate. Lot thirty-one."

"That's a damned odd place for lawyers' offices. But you produced the divorce papers when you went to register your marriage to Tom Richards."

"That's the oddest thing. I couldn't find them anywhere. I asked Gary and he said he gave them to me and I must have lost

93

them. My passport was still in my maiden name and Bunchie said that and my birth certificate would be enough."

"Didn't you go to the lawyer and ask for a copy?"

"Bunchie said there was no need to bother."

"When Gary gave you the ten thousand, where did he get it from? Did he have a safe?"

"Nothing like that. He just produced an envelope. He said he wanted the house for himself."

"And where did Bunchie really meet you?"

"At the supermarket. I knew the money wouldn't last all that long these days. I got a room at the Y."

"Amy, think carefully. Gary did not earn much as a copper. How could he be getting extra money?"

"I dunno. He kept telling me he was doing a lot of overtime." Amy waved her slim arm and a heavy silver bracelet with several objects dangling from it flashed in the electric light.

"Here's an odd thing. May I see your bracelet?"

"Okay. I had a friend make it up for me. She's ever so clever. She just uses all little odd bits of silver."

94

Agatha studied the bracelet carefully, turning it in her fingers. "There's a key here," she said. "An odd-shaped key. It looks like my bank deposit key."

"Well, I never."

"Where did Gary bank?"

"I think it was at the Mircester and General."

"Did Gary make a will?"

"Yes, I've got a copy of it somewhere. It's one of those wills you do yourself. He left everything to me, but under my maiden name, Amy Tubb. He said he made it out just before we got married."

"And your passport is still in your maiden name?"

"Yes, I never got around to changing it."

"Right. Get your coat. We'll try the bank first. Bring the will and the death certificate and your passport."

Agatha waited impatiently while Amy teetered about on her high heels, opening and shutting drawers. Eventually she found everything in a file in the bottom drawer of her husband's desk.

CHAPTER FIVE

Once in the office, relieved to find it deserted except for Mrs. Freedman, Toni turned to the secretary. "Mrs. Freedman, I've given Agatha a month's notice. Should I type out a letter?"

"Oh, dear. If she knows, then I don't think you should bother. Where will you go?"

"Probably to another detective agency or maybe to the police."

Mrs. Freedman peered over her spectacles at Toni. "There isn't another agency around to match this one. If you join one of the lesser ones, it'll be dogsbody work, you being so young. Then, there's the police. Off to Hendon or somewhere for training. Maybe refused on the grounds of your colour."

"What?"

"One of my nephews got turned down. Gloucester police have to take a quota of Asians and Jamaicans and so on. Ethnic diversity, it's called. He's with the transport police in London now. Even if you got a job here, don't judge them by Bill Wong. Lot of chauvinist pigs, that's what they are. If you keep them off, they'll damn you as a lesbian and start putting nasty things in your locker."

"Mrs. Freedman, I think your loyalty to Agatha is why you are making things up."

"Yes, loyalty's a great thing," said Mrs. Freedman. She put her glasses back on her small nose and began typing again.

Agatha rang Toni and told her that she was with Amy and that they would meet her in the square. Although she felt there was no need for the girl to come along, Agatha was determined to involve her whenever anything that looked important came up, in the hope that Toni might change her mind and stay on.

"Where are we going?" asked Toni breathlessly as she got into the backseat of Agatha's car.

"The Mircester and General Bank," said Agatha. She explained rapidly about the key.

They all got out of the car and entered the bank, which stood between two shuttered shops. More failed businesses, thought Agatha. Town high streets are dying and all because we've become lazy and prefer to do our shopping in one go at one of the big supermarkets on the outskirts. It was also the fault of various councils who had a penchant for turning high streets into pedestrian areas and then charging high fees for parking at the nearest available car park. No one wanted to walk anymore carrying heavy bags of groceries and moving from little shop to little shop. Maybe in the end, high streets would be turned into museums with people in twentieth-century dress parading up and down.

Agatha asked to speak to the manager. They were told to wait.

Snow began to patter against the high windows. I should have bought snow tyres, mourned Agatha, but they'd take so long to arrive at the garage, and surely spring would come soon.

At last they were summoned to the manager's office. He was small, balding and fussy.

After Amy had explained her visit, he examined the will, the passport and the key with maddening slowness, occasionally shaking his head and murmuring, "Dear, dear."

Agatha, who had been painfully trying to practice tolerance, burst out with, "What?

What's taking you so long? How long are we supposed to sit here waiting while you procrastinate?"

"I have tae be sure," he said crossly. "There are a lot o' bad, bad people about. Oh, yes."

"You're not from Auchtermurchy, or one of these godforsaken places?"

"I am from Stornoway and proud o' it. I will get Gladys to take ye to the safe deposit box." He pressed a buzzer on his desk.

A blonde, so pale she looked as if she had been bleached all over, told them to follow her. They descended stairs to a cavernous basement. Gladys opened one of the doors with two keys.

"What is the number of the box?" she asked.

"I don't know," wailed Amy.

Back up the stairs again to wait for the manager, Mr. Macleod. Then much humming and hawing and form signing before the number was released. Gladys appeared again like a pale ghost leading them to the nether regions. "You just shut the outside door behind you when you leave," she said. "It will lock automatically." She pulled out the box and set it on a metal table in the middle of the room and then left them to it. Agatha drew out three pairs of latex gloves and said they'd better put them on.

"Here, you do it." Amy handed Agatha the key.

Agatha unlocked the box and opened the lid.

The three women stared down at the contents in amazement. There were four passports, all in different names but all bearing the late Gary Beech's photograph. A pair of underpants, which Agatha unwrapped, revealed a small pistol. All that was left in the box was a small leather bag with a drawstring top. Toni opened it and peered in and then shook some of the contents out on her hand.

"Pebbles," said Amy bitterly. "What's he doing putting nasty dirty stones in a safe deposit box?"

"Wait a bit," said Toni excitedly. "I think they're uncut diamonds. I saw a programme on diamonds, and this is what they look like in the raw. We'd better take them to the police. They could be conflict diamonds."

"What are you talking about?" demanded Agatha crossly, forgetting that she had resolved to be sweetness and light to Toni on every occasion.

"Conflict diamonds or blood diamonds are used to fund rebel groups in places like Sierra Leone or Angola."

"But what on earth would a village copper be doing getting involved in anything at all going on in Africa?" asked Agatha.

"Probably nothing," said Toni. "Maybe just a criminal payoff for something. We'd better take this lot to the police."

"Must we?" said Amy. "I mean, if they're rough, they could be polished up by a jeweller friend of mine."

"No," said Agatha firmly. "They've got to be examined by the police."

Amy's eyes were suddenly as hard as the uncut diamonds. "First, it's my property, see? I'm taking it and that's that."

"We'll have to report it nonetheless," said Toni.

"Don't rate your lives very high, do you?" sneered Amy.

"You knew what Gary was up to all along," said Agatha. "Out with it!"

"Get stuffed. You're fired." Amy swept everything into a capacious handbag and marched out.

"Right," said Agatha as Amy flagged down a cab outside the bank. "We'd better get to police headquarters."

"I think we should follow her," said Toni.

"Why? She's got a cosy marriage with a rich husband."

"I think she only married him because he

101

was rich, and it does appear he's a bit of a bastard."

Agatha wanted to argue but remembered in time that Toni's value as a detective was often her clear and practical view of things. "All right," she said. "Let's see what she's going to do."

But when they arrived at Amy's house, her car had gone and the house had an empty air.

They waited an hour or so, and then Toni said, "I think, after all, we'd better go to the police. My bet is she's not going near that husband of hers."

Agatha was sick and tired of being interrogated by the time she left the police station and dropped Toni off at her flat. The gritters had been out, as a supply of salt had arrived from abroad, so she was able to make it back to her cottage without slipping. There was a note for her on the kitchen table from Charles: "Can't stand this beastly weather. Gone to the South of France. Luv, Charles."

Agatha, still worried about Toni, felt lonely. She called the vicarage but was told that Mrs. Bloxby was visiting a relative in Bexhill in Sussex. She then phoned Roy Silver to see whether he would like to visit at the week-end, but he said he was going to a simply fabulous party and wouldn't be free.

Her cats were sleeping peacefully. The house seemed unnaturally quiet.

She felt in the need of action. There was a bag of empty cans of various sorts on the kitchen floor, along with a crate of empty bottles. The council had supplied house-holders with black boxes for the tin cans and the bottles, but Agatha had lost both. She would take them down to Tesco's supermarket in Stow-on-the-Wold and dump the lot in their special bins and then draw some money from the hole in the wall. The snow was light and looked as if it were about to slacken off. A thin disk of a moon was appearing behind the clouds. The village of Carsely was shrouded in snow, wrapped in snow and wrapped in silence. Agatha glanced at her watch. It was just after midnight.

She drove down to the back of the supermarket. The bottles went into the bins with the satisfying sound of breaking glass. Must be a hooligan inside all of us, thought Agatha.

Then she got rid of the tin cans. She drove carefully round to the cash machine, bumping over the ruts of frozen snow. Supermarket car parks were private property, and she had been told that if they cleared them themselves and someone slipped and fell, they would have to pay compensation. *But* if someone slipped and fell in the uncleared car park, it was their own bloody fault.

She parked in front of the cash machine. Beside the cash machine and beyond a stack of supermarket trolleys were two rides for small children. One periodically emitted bursts of supposedly childish laughter, but Agatha thought it sounded more like malicious elves watching someone come to grief.

She drew out a hundred pounds and was just tucking it away in her wallet when her eye caught what looked like a heap of clothes lying between the two small rides for children.

Why me? wondered Agatha. If that's some drunk sleeping it off, I'll need to get help for the poor sod.

She walked round the row of trolleys and bent down. Whoever it was was completely covered by a blanket. Agatha pulled the blanket away from the face.

The moon shone down. The hellish children's voices cackled out. And Agatha stared down at the dead face of Amy Richards.

Inside the supermarket, although it was

closed, she could see the shelf stackers at work.

She hammered on the glass doors. Faces turned towards her. A security man came to the door and waved at her to go away.

Agatha took out her notebook and printed in large letters: DEAD BODY IN CAR PARK.

105

CHAPTER SIX

Agatha had to stop the security guard from trying to resuscitate Amy. "Leave her," she yelled, dragging him off. "Any idiot can see she's stone dead. You're tampering with evidence."

Feeling sick and shaken, Agatha, who had phoned the police, heard the wail of sirens, and then police cars, marked and unmarked, poured into the car park. A grim-faced policewoman whom Agatha did not know began to question her and then said she was to go in a police car to headquarters and wait there to make a statement.

Agatha phoned her lawyer, a mild man called inappropriately Bill Sykes, and told him to meet her at headquarters. Agatha had previously used him to make out her will. He protested that he did not handle criminal law, to which Agatha snapped, "Then get down here and learn."

Agatha ploughed on through the questioning with little help from her timid, sleepy lawyer. She had taken the precaution of summoning him, knowing well that the police would consider this one coincidence too far — that she had suddenly decided to dump trash in the middle of the night after watching Amy's house and had conveniently found her dead body. Over and over her story she went while the asthmatic clock on the wall above her head wheezed out the minutes.

At last, she held up her hand. "Do you mind telling me how she died?"

Wilkes, who had been conducting the interview, scowled at her. A thickset detective sergeant by the name of Briggs asked nastily, "Don't you know?"

"If I knew, I wouldn't be asking you," howled Agatha.

"As far as we can gather, she was stabbed through the heart," said Wilkes.

"What with?" asked Agatha.

"What do you think?" asked Briggs sarcastically.

Mr. Sykes, the lawyer, was tired. He found a reserve of bad-tempered courage he did not know he possessed.

"Answer Mrs. Raisin's question," he snapped, "and stop wasting time with your bullying."

Briggs looked as if a rabbit had just bitten him in the ankle. Wilkes said heavily, "Some thin-bladed knife, we think."

"Are you charging my client with anything?" said little Mr. Sykes, glaring through his thick glasses.

"Not at this moment," said Briggs heavily.

"Then you are free to leave, Mrs. Raisin," said Mr. Sykes, wrapping a long muffler around his neck. "Come along."

"Hold yourself ready for more questioning," Wilkes called after their retreating backs.

Outside the interview room, Agatha hugged the startled Mr. Sykes. "Oh, well done. I am so tired, I didn't know how to stand up to them, and believe me, that's something that hardly ever happens to me."

"Where is your car?" asked Mr. Sykes.

"I left it at the supermarket."

"I shall take you there. And," said Mr. Sykes, quite overcome by the memory of his own bravery, "you can smoke if you like."

When they got to the car park, a tent had been erected over the body. But all Agatha wanted to do was to get home and go to sleep. She thanked her lawyer again, got into her car and set off over the whitened landscape. The snow had ceased, and the road down into Carsely was slippery again. She cruised down it in second gear, finally turning into Lilac Lane with a sigh of relief.

As she climbed out of her car, she found her knees were trembling. She clicked the lock on the car. She heard a voice call, "Agatha!"

She swung round. The moon had disappeared behind a bank of clouds, and she saw a tall, dark figure approaching her. She was just opening her mouth to scream when a once loved voice said, "Are you all right? I heard about the murder on the radio."

"James?" said Agatha in a wondering voice. "Is it really you?"

"Who else?" replied her ex-husband, James Lacey.

"Oh, I am so glad to see you," said Agatha, and burst into tears.

Inside Agatha's cottage, James waited patiently in the kitchen while Agatha fled upstairs to repair her make-up. He looked just the same, she thought, with his thick hair going only a little grey at the sides and those intense blue eyes of his.

Satisfied at last that she had done as much to her face as was possible, she sprayed on Coco Mademoiselle and went down the stairs.

"When did you get back?" she asked.

"Today . . . late. I was listening to the radio news when I learned a body had been found in the car park at Tesco's supermarket. I thought it better to wait in Carsely for you to get back rather than miss you on the road. I've poured you a brandy. I suppose hot sweet tea would have been better, but you look as if you need something to cheer you up."

Agatha nodded. He went through to the sitting room and returned with a goblet of brandy. Agatha took a gulp and smiled at him mistily. "It's very good to see you. It seems I am now the number one suspect in the murder of Amy Richards."

"If you're not too tired, tell me about it."

"I would like to," said Agatha. "I'm exhausted, but too strung up and nervous to sleep. Oh, I should have phoned Toni. They'll have questioned her as well. Toni's another problem. I'll tell you all about it."

James produced a small notebook and pen while Agatha talked and talked. He occasionally made notes.

When she had finished, James prompted,

"You said there was some trouble with Toni. What is it?"

Wearily, Agatha outlined the situation and finished by saying plaintively, "Don't look so severe. I've made a mess of things and I don't know what to do."

"Simon was very young," remarked James. "And he certainly didn't have undying love for Toni or he wouldn't have fallen for this new girl so easily. The trouble is that you cannot possibly do anything about it. Toni will need to make her own mistakes from now on. She may come round. She is, you know, fiercely independent."

"But she's so young!"

"As you were once, Agatha, and I bet you were a bulldozer compared to Toni. I could try to have a word with her."

"Would you? She always respected you."

"Now, you'd best get off to bed. We'll meet tomorrow, say, for lunch at the George. Have a long lie-in. I'll phone the office for you."

"Where have you been?"

"I still write travel books, but I've moved on to the large glossy type, exploring more remote parts of the world."

"Are there any remote parts left? I thought even the top of Everest was getting over-crowded."

"Oh, there are a few places. Lock up after me and go to bed."

When he had gone and Agatha was drifting off to sleep, she was glad to find her old obsession for him had not returned. But I'm so weary of being on my own, she thought. Charles is like my cats, self-sufficient, and Roy would drop me like a shot if he got a good PR assignment.

But Agatha got only a few hours' sleep. She was awakened at nine o'clock by her cleaner, Doris Simpson, telling her that Bill Wong and some female detective were downstairs waiting to talk to her.

Agatha gloomily surveyed her face in the bathroom mirror. She applied a cream that was supposed to remove bags and dark circles from under her eyes. It didn't work. She put on a thick layer of make-up and decided she looked awful. Why was foundation cream either ghostly white or brown? She washed off the whole lot and put on a thin layer of tinted moisturiser instead. She could hear water dripping from the thatch on her cottage roof. A thaw had set in.

Wearing a pink cotton blouson over cashmere slacks, she started down the stairs, remembering only on the bottom step that she hated pink.

Bill and Alice were in the kitchen. Doris had served them coffee and biscuits.

"Sit down, Agatha," said Bill.

"Of course I'm going to sit down," said Agatha crossly. "It's my own bloody house. I can sit on the damned chimney if I feel like it."

"I know you're tired," said Alice soothingly. "But we would like to go over a few points again."

"Wait until I get a black coffee and a cigarette," said Agatha grumpily.

"By the way," said Bill, "Toni's dropped the charges against Paul Finlay."

Toni was already awake and getting carefully dressed for an interview with Mixden, a rival detective agency. Dressed in a neat tailored trouser suit, worn under a scarlet puffa jacket, she set out.

Mixden was located on the outskirts of Mircester. She drove out through the slushy roads, trying to fight down an odd feeling of disloyalty to Agatha. Agatha had behaved disgracefully, she told herself as she parked in front of a square pebbledash building with the legend MIXDEN over the front door.

She recognised the receptionist as a girl she had gone to school with — Chelsea Flitter — although Chelsea had become a blonde and was wearing such thick make-up, she looked like a character from a Japanese Noh production.

"Hiya, Tone," she said. "Coming to join us?"

"Maybe."

"You're to go right in. Mr. Mixden is through that door on the right. Have a chat when you come out. We should get together."

Toni nodded and walked through into Mr. Mixden's office. He was a very small man with thin hair combed over his bald patch, where it lay in oiled streaks like seaweed on a rock at low tide. He had gold-rimmed glasses, a large nose and a wide mouth turned down at the corners. He smiled at Toni, revealing a pair of dazzlingly white dentures, and waved her into a chair opposite his desk.

"You're as pretty as your photos," he said. "You've had quite a bit of publicity for so young a lady. Why do you want to join us?"

"I feel I've been getting stale working for the one agency," said Toni. "Agatha Raisin has been very good to me, but she feels she has a right to control my private life as well as my work."

"I see." He made a rapid note on a pad in

front of him. Then he looked across at her. "The Raisin agency is very successful. So you could be of great use to us and earn a lot of money into the bargain. First of all, how do I know you are not here just to act as a spy and report the cases we have and then try to get the Raisin woman to take them away from us?"

"I would not even dream of it," said Toni evenly, to hide her rising temper.

He tapped the pencil on the pad. "We could look at it another way. You could go on working for La Raisin and report to us on her cases. That way you could earn double. What do you say?"

Toni simply rose to her feet and walked straight out the door, slamming it behind her. She got into her car and sat there for a moment, feeling small and grubby.

The wind howled about her small car. She could hardly believe that Mixden had suggested such a thing. Well, courage! There was one other detective agency, FindIT, in the centre of town. Surely with her record they would be glad to get her.

She parked her car in the main square, trying to fight off the uneasy feeling that she was being watched.

James Lacey had gone into Mircester that

morning to shop for some new winter boots. Along the narrow street in front of him, he recognised Toni's blond head. Then he noticed that as she occasionally turned, as if suspecting she was watched, a man with a beard dived into a doorway.

James followed and phoned Agatha, keeping an eye all the time on Toni. Agatha had just reached her office when she got James's call on her mobile. "It'll be that sod Paul Finlay," she said. "I'll be right over."

"No, stay where you are," said James. "He'll recognise you."

James remembered Agatha telling him about Paul Finlay the night before. But surely the man would not attack Toni in broad daylight and on a busy street. Toni turned in at the entrance to the FindIT detective agency.

The bearded man went into a café opposite and took a seat by the window. James followed him in.

Inside the agency, there was no reception desk, only a waiting room with easy chairs and a low coffee table.

Toni was just beginning to wonder how to get hold of anyone when a door at the side opened and a tall woman asked, "Can I help you?"

The woman was mannish, with thick grey hair worn in a French pleat. Her eyes were very large and black, and her nose curved over a thin mouth. She was wearing a purple sweater, so tight that it revealed pendulous breasts underneath. She reminded Toni of a witch she had seen pictured in a children's book.

"I am looking for a job," said Toni.

"Ah, yes, Miss Gilmour. I recognise you. Fallen out with our dear Agatha?"

"I would like to see the boss," said Toni firmly.

"I am the boss, my sweeting. Not a very good detective, are you? My name is Dolores Watchman. Come into my office."

Said the spider to the fly, thought Toni. There was something overpowering and quite threatening about Dolores.

The office was tastefully decorated. Dolores sat behind an antique mahogany desk. Toni sat in an upright chair in front of it. There were several of what looked like good abstracts on the wall and a framed print of an Aubrey Beardsley drawing.

Dolores lit a cigar and leaned back in her chair. "So when did you and Aggie split up?"

"We didn't . . . we haven't," said Toni. "I wanted a change of scene."

"I don't mind giving you a trial for a few

117

months. Like a drink?"

"No, thank you. A bit early for me."

"Never too early for me." Dolores opened a bottom drawer in her desk and took out a bottle of whisky and a glass.

Toni laughed. "I thought detectives only did that in books."

"Get one thing straight, my child, you *never* laugh at me. I demand absolute respect. Now I'll start you with the small stuff and see how you get on. You cannot expect me to pay you a full salary until I decide you are worth it."

"I've made a mistake," said Toni, getting abruptly to her feet. "Good day."

"Why, you snotty little bitch!" shouted Dolores as Toni darted out the door, out of the office and out into the street.

James saw Toni emerge from the office opposite just as the man he was sure must be Paul Finlay threw down some money for his bill and exited the café. Paul followed Toni, and James followed both.

Toni was standing, irresolute, beside her car when a voice behind her said, "This is Paul. I have a knife. Get into your car. If you scream, I will kill you."

The next thing that happened was a shriek rending the air. James had twisted Paul's knife arm backwards so viciously that he had dislocated Paul's shoulder. Paul fell to the ground, shouting and writhing in pain. James called the police. "If you try anything again," he hissed at Paul, "I'll break your neck."

James sat in the reception area of police headquarters and waited for Toni to emerge. He had stopped Agatha from coming, saying it would be better if he had a word with Toni on his own.

At last she emerged, followed by Bill. "I'm just going to take her for a drink," said James. "I'm sure she needs one."

"All right," said Bill. "You do suddenly seem to pop up at the right moment. Seen Agatha?"

"Of course."

When they were seated in the pub, Toni thanked James for having rescued her.

"I think you should phone Agatha and take the rest of the day off," said James. He added gently, "You know, Agatha is terribly upset about the mistake she made regarding Simon Black. She had no right to interfere in your life, and she knows that now. She had one of her intuitions about Simon. Probably wrong. Can't you withdraw your notice and just get on with her?"

"I'll have to," said Toni miserably. She told James about her attempts to find work at two other agencies.

"There you are," said James. "There's worse than Agatha around."

Toni gave a weak laugh.

"That's my girl. Tell her you've decided to stay."

"All right. What if she tells me to get lost?"

"Agatha's too bighearted to do that. Also, she does appreciate your work."

Toni finished her drink. "I'll get right back to the office and do it now."

"Before you go, maybe you can help me. I have to buy a toy for a friend's child — a little girl, seven years old. What do you suggest?"

"There's a great shop run by May Dinwoody. All the toys are handmade. You'll find it in Tapestry Lane. It was Simon's idea, but it was Agatha who did a big publicity stunt on it."

The days of May Dinwoody's poverty had gone, but she had not acquired any dress sense. She was wearing a long cardigan over a pink T-shirt, a tweed skirt and Wellington boots decorated with pink daisies.

She mostly worked over the books in an

office at the back of the shop, but when she saw the handsome figure of James entering the shop, she decided to serve him herself. He explained what he was looking for. "People usually buy dolls for little girls," said May in her soft Scottish burr, "but sometimes they are not dolly-type girls."

James laughed. "She is a bit of a tomboy."

"Let me see. What about this?"

She picked up a beautifully handcrafted wooden black-and-white spaniel. "You pull it along by its leash," said May. "Listen!" She placed the toy on the floor and pulled the leash. The dog's eyes lit up, and it said in a rasping voice, "Walk me."

"And you see," said May eagerly, "it can become more demanding if you don't move it."

"I said walk me *now*," growled the dog.

"The little switch under the red collar turns it on and off," explained May.

The price seemed terribly steep to James, but on the other hand, he knew the little girl would be delighted. As May wrapped it up, James said, "I believe you know my friend Agatha Raisin?"

"Yes indeed. I owe everything to Agatha and that young man Simon Black. It was Simon who suggested that she publicise my toys. I felt a bittie guilty because I thought she demanded a harsh price."

"For publicising you? That doesn't sound like Agatha."

"Oh, no, she refused to charge a penny. It was at my flat in Oddley Croesus that I heard her talking to Simon when I went to the kitchen to make tea. She said, 'I just want to remind you that I am doing this so that you will leave Toni alone for three years. She is too young to get seriously involved with anyone.' You can imagine my relief when I got an invitation to Simon's wedding and he is marrying an army girl. So it looks as if he might have been the fickle type all along."

James nodded, but he felt depressed. Agatha had behaved disgracefully. Her famous intuition had not been involved. She had merely wanted to keep a good detective.

When he met Agatha for lunch, her face was glowing. "Toni's decided to stay," she said. "Isn't that marvellous?"

"I've just been buying a toy for a friend's little daughter at May Dinwoody's," said James. Agatha quickly raised the menu to cover her face, but he leaned across the table and pulled it away. Agatha gave him a hunted look from out of her bearlike eyes.

"So it seems," said James acidly, "that you

122

exacted a pretty steep price out of Simon for helping the Dinwoody woman."

"I thought it was the best thing to do," howled Agatha with all the ferocity of the really guilty.

"You were cruel and selfish. What are you having to eat?"

"What do you want me to eat? Humble pie? Look. I'm sorry, sorry, sorry. Do you want me to go away?"

"Oddly enough, no. Did you hear about my rescue of Toni?"

"Yes, she told me. I wish it could have been me. Make amends in a way, you know."

"Just as well it wasn't. Now, let's order something and decide what we're going to do about your murders."

They were sitting at a table on a terrace at the back of the hotel overlooking the garden. Spring had come at last as March went out like a lamb. The hotel garden was heavy with the scent of blossom. A pale disc of a sun rose through tiny ragged little dark clouds above their heads. It was a place and a night for lovers, thought Agatha gloomily: not for one shamed female detective facing her ex across the table.

"I gather," said Agatha, "that whoever killed Gary Beech ransacked his house. They were desperately looking for something. I think Amy was killed because she knew too much, or they suspected she might have known something."

"Did she look as if she had been tortured?" asked James.

"I only looked at her face. It was unmarked and peaceful — dead peaceful, if you know what I mean. She hadn't been strangled. I didn't touch the body or turn it over. Then police said she had been stabbed."

"Did Gary Beech leave a will?" asked James.

"Yes. He left everything to Amy." She pulled out her mobile and dialled Patrick. When she rang off, she said, "No further news. There are the diamonds, of course. That's probably what they were looking for. Maybe Amy put the house up for sale. The police have surely finished with it."

"Let's just enjoy our dinner, go home and change, and then we'll break in."

Agatha grinned happily. "Quite like old times."

CHAPTER SEVEN

They had decided to set off at two in the morning. As Agatha got ready, wearing a dark blue blouse and black trousers, she wished with all her heart that she had never interfered in Toni's life. James had been pleasant over lunch, but there was a certain coldness and reserve about him. He had forgiven her a lot in the past. She wondered now if he would ever forgive her for her behaviour that had driven off young Simon.

"Creepy," was James's comment as they drove into Winter Parva.

"I think it's because there are no trees or gardens," said Agatha. "The houses front straight onto the high street. You have to drive right through the village to the far end. Yes. Now make a right, a left and a right again. It's that cottage at the end separated from the others by a bit. Patrick gave me directions."

"No point in advertising our presence. I'll

park in that field under the trees and walk."

A FOR SALE sign glimmered whitely outside Beech's cottage. "We could, of course," whispered Agatha nervously, "have simply gone to the estate agent tomorrow and asked for the keys."

"Might not work," said James. "There's a recession on and they're desperate for sales and would probably send someone to show us around. No, we won't go in the front gate. Go along outside the side of the garden and then we'll climb over the fence."

Which Toni could probably have leapt in one bound, thought Agatha.

"Right," said James in a low voice. "Over here and we can try to get in through the conservatory at the back."

Agatha tried to scale the high wooden fence but fell backwards onto the ground.

"I'll give you a boost," said James. He held out his clasped hands, and Agatha gingerly placed one foot in them. He gave a great heave. Up she went and over, landing, winded, on grass on the other side.

"That was dangerous," grumbled Agatha. "What if it had been a greenhouse I landed on?"

"Stop wittering. We've got work to do."

James went up to the conservatory door. He took out a pencil torch and flashed a beam at the lock. He took out a thin piece of metal and inserted it between the lock and the doorjamb. There was a satisfying click as the door sprang open.

They eased their way quietly inside, and James closed the door behind them. The place had all been cleaned up. Whatever plants there had been in the conservatory had been removed.

They moved from room to room. Agatha could not see any of the expensive pieces of furniture that Bill had mentioned. Amy must have sold them.

"There are no drawers or anything left to search," she muttered dismally. "Where could he have hidden something that neither the police nor his killers could find? The garden?"

"It's been all dug over. The police will have searched there as well."

"I wonder if there's a loft. People often hide things up in lofts."

They felt their way up the stairs in the darkness. The upper floor contained two bedrooms, a bathroom and a cupboard with a hot-water boiler. James shone his torch at the ceiling. "No evidence of any loft."

"Nothing but fake olde world beams on the ceiling. How naff," said Agatha.

"Now there's an interesting thing." James

studied the beams. "He might have made a hollow in one of those beams to cache something."

"I don't see how he could have done that without leaving some trace," said Agatha. "Oh, let's get out of here."

"You can go and wait in the car if you like."

"Not on my own. I'll stay here until you are finished. I mean, James, they're not thick original beams. They're just really slats made to look like beams."

"Wait a minute." James got down on his knees and began to delicately run his hands along the skirting board.

Agatha sat on the floor, feeling sore after her crash over the fence. "If I wanted to hide something in the skirting board," she said wearily, "it would probably be behind my bed."

"There's a thought. I wonder which room he slept in."

"The bigger of the two, I suppose," said Agatha nervously. "Can't we just leave?"

"Not long now."

James went into the larger bedroom. There were two closets in the right-hand wall. He was just making for them when they heard a car coming along the road and lights shone across the ceiling. He took a quick look out of the window. "It's the police. Damn it. Someone must have seen us. Let's get into that closet and hope when they find the doors locked that they'll go away."

The closet they crowded into had once been used as a wardrobe. A few steel hangers hung from a rod.

Then they heard the voices of the police outside the house. "Looks all locked up," said one voice. "Try round the back, Harry."

There was a silence and then Harry's voice. "Locked up round the back. Shall we leave it?"

They were joined by a woman. "I was walking my dog and I'll swear I saw two people going up the side of the house."

"What were you doing walking your dog at this time of night?" demanded the policeman called Harry.

"I couldn't sleep right, not after that horrible murder, I couldn't," she said.

"Better phone it in," said Harry's companion.

"What are you doing?" demanded Agatha as James switched on his torch.

"Still desperately trying to find something that might make them forgive us if they find us. There's something down here on the floor."

Harry's voice sounded. "They've roused

the estate agent. He'll be along in a minute or two with the keys."

"Sunk," said Agatha.

"There's this odd knothole thing. I wonder if I push . . ."

The back of the closet slid open, revealing a small room beyond. "It's like Narnia — *The Lion, the Witch and the Wardrobe*," said James excitedly. "We can hide in here until they're gone."

They sat down on the floor, huddled together, after he had shut them in. Agatha's hormones gave a treacherous lurch. Not now, she told them.

After what seemed an age but was only a quarter of an hour, they heard the arrival of the estate agent. Then the unlocking of the front door and the clump of policemen's boots. Then came the fretful voice of what Agatha guessed was the estate agent. "It's no use looking for fingerprints or foot-prints," she said. "I don't know how many people have been through this house, and believe me, they all turned out to be ghouls, wanted to look at a house where a murder had been committed."

Footsteps came up the stairs and into the bedroom.

"Oh, God, I'm going to sneeze," said Agatha.

James twisted her face round and kissed her full on the mouth. Her senses reeled. She faintly heard a voice say, "Nothing here."

"Why, James!" said Agatha softly.

"Anything to shut you up," he muttered.

Agatha's hormones packed up their bags and left again.

They waited until the police had left the house, waited while they heard the complaints of the estate agent for having been dragged out in the middle of the night, waited while the dog-walking woman grumbled her way off down the lane, frightened to move until the police car drove off.

"Now," said James, switching on the torch. "What have we here?"

"There's a light switch," said Agatha, "and no windows. We could risk switching it on."

James went to the switch in the wall. A naked light bulb shone down on them.

Both of them looked around. The tiny secret room contained only a crumpled sleeping bag in one corner and, beside it, a ledger. "We could take this home and read it in comfort," said Agatha.

"No," replied James sharply. "Got your gloves on? Good. We take a quick look and then, somehow, we've got to let the police know where to look for it."

131

James gingerly opened the ledger. "It's in some sort of code or something," he said. "I should have a brought a camera. I know, let's get out of here and borrow it for a bit. It means we'll have to sneak back here and replace it. We'll need to make sure there's not a trace of a fingerprint or footprint. Damn, that really is messing up any police evidence. Well, we got this far and they didn't. Might just photograph the thing and post it to them."

Agatha agreed. She felt it was wrong, but on the other hand, to notify the police meant explaining that they had broken into Gary Beech's house.

James was wearing a dark leather jerkin and had the ledger zipped up inside it. "Don't you think," whispered Agatha plaintively, "that there might be a back door to this garden?"

"I suppose there might be," said James, wondering why on earth he hadn't thought of it before.

They made their way quietly out of the house. James risked flashing his torch around the garden. "There's a gate at the end over there, but it's going to be the same problem. It's solid and it's as high as the fence. It's padlocked."

"Can't you pick the lock?"

"It'll take a few moments. It's a pity you're not more agile. We could just have shinned over it. You should get that hip replacement."

Agatha remained mulishly quiet while he got to work picking the lock. She did not like anyone, particularly James, knowing that she had been operated on for a hip replacement. Also, she was stiff and sore from getting over the fence. At last the padlock clicked open. James let Agatha out into the lane at the back, relocked the padlock and climbed nimbly over the fence.

"Now, if we go quietly along this lane at the backs of the houses, we should reach my car. That way there's no fear of someone in the houses seeing us."

"Someone could be looking out of a back window."

"Too many trees and bushes at the back, and I can't see a light in a window anywhere. *Come on.*"

Agatha was so grateful to be finally back in her cottage kitchen. "Coffee would be nice," said James.

"A stiff gin and tonic would be nicer," said Agatha.

"Well, make a strong coffee for me. I'll nip next door and get my camera. Don't

133

touch that ledger with your bare hands!" James was Agatha's nearest neighbour.

When James returned, Agatha had moved to her living room and was stretched out on the sofa asleep, a glass of gin and tonic perilously balanced on her chest and a smouldering cigarette in one hand.

He gently removed her drink and stubbed out her cigarette. He decided to leave her to sleep while he had a look in the ledger himself.

The entries in the ledger were baffling. There were long lines of columns with cryptic entries such a c.h. b. P.L., t. r. P.L. and so on in the same style. He woke Agatha, who blinked up at him and then came fully awake, crying, "What did you find?"

"Nothing but a lot of gobbledygook. Come and have a look before I photograph the pages. There are only about five pages of entries. If this is what the killers were looking for, then I wonder why they wasted their time."

Agatha followed him into the kitchen and stared in bafflement at the entries.

"Now what do we do?" she asked.

"I photograph all the entries and then, so help me, I've got to take the book back, make sure the place is swept clean so there's no trace of our visit and then drop an anonymous line to the police."

Agatha awoke the next morning with the feel of James's lips burning into her memory. In his way, he had been passionate in bed when they were married, but somehow only during the sex act itself. When it was over, he had rolled over to his side of the bed and gone to sleep as if she didn't exist. Agatha tried to erase her feelings over the kiss by remembering how awful the marriage had been: all his infuriating persnickety bachelor ways such as complaining about the laundry, trying to forbid her to work. She gave herself a mental shake. She did not want to end up in the miserable depths of an obsession for James again.

But in its way, obsession was as necessary to Agatha Raisin as drink to an alcoholic. In the way that an alcoholic will endlessly chase the dream of when drink brought pleasure and escape, Agatha usually remembered only the beginning of obsessions, when the days were brighter and she felt young again.

She wondered whether to call on James before she went to the office but steeled herself against the urge.

Agatha was just about to leave her cottage after letting her cats out into the back garden for the day when the postman arrived with a large parcel. "Grand day," said the postman.

Agatha could almost smell the countryside coming to life after the bitter winter. The sky above was pale blue, and somewhere nearby a blackbird poured down its song.

It was on mornings like this that Agatha realised why she loved living in the Cotswolds so much. Perhaps, she thought, there is nowhere more beautiful in Britain than this man-made piece of England with its thatched cottages and gardens crammed with flowers.

The parcel was very heavy. She heaved it in and onto the kitchen table. It was addressed to her in block capitals. There was no return address.

She stared down at it, wondering at the same time if James had been successful in returning the ledger and somehow telling the police about the secret room without revealing their identities.

Agatha took a sharp knife out of the kitchen drawer and sliced the tape that sealed the parcel. Just before she wrenched it open, she paused. What if it were a bomb?

She put her ear to the parcel and then told herself she was being silly. Surely bombs ticked only in old movies.

She was reminded of some old game show on television where people would shout either "Don't open the box!" or "Open the box!"

She tore open the top flaps. Whatever was in there was covered in bubble wrap. She gingerly opened the coverings and then stared down at the revealed contents. Rigid with shock, she looked into the dead eyes of Gary Beech. His face was encrusted with little pellets of ice. The head had been frozen.

She sank down into a chair and grasped her knees to stop them from shaking.

Agatha felt she did not have enough strength to get up and call the police from the phone on the kitchen counter. She reached up and pulled her handbag down from the kitchen table and fished out her mobile and dialled 999.

James looked out of his window and saw police cars and a forensic unit arriving outside. He rushed out of doors in time to see a white-faced Agatha being led out and ushered into a police car.

He tried to get to her but had his way blocked by a policeman. "Can't go there, sir," he said.

"Agatha!" shouted James. "What's up?"

"Head!" screamed Agatha wildly as she was thrust into the car, which then sped off, and the road in front of her cottage was taped off.

Agatha, who had refused offers of treatment for shock and simply wanted to get any interview over with, told Inspector Wilkes about the arrival of the package. While she making her statement in a weak, faltering voice quite unlike her own, the interview was suddenly suspended as Wilkes was summoned from the room.

She waited, staring blankly into space, reviving only enough to refuse a policewoman's offer of hot sweet tea.

Wilkes eventually returned. His face was grim. "Do you know there was a note for you with the head?"

"Too much of a shock to look further," said Agatha. "What did it say?"

"It says, 'You're next, you nosy bitch, if you keep on interfering.' What have you been up to?"

Agatha thought wildly of her visit to Gary Beech's home. She said, "I was investigating his death at the request of his ex-wife. . . ."

"Who you found murdered?"

"Yes."

"And?"

"That's all."

"Have you found out anything at all you are not telling us? You see, we got an anonymous call at dawn, telling us about a secret room in Gary Beech's house. You wouldn't know about that, would you?"

"A secret room!" exclaimed Agatha. "That sounds like something out of Enid Blyton. It would never cross my mind." She leaned forward wearily. "Do you know yet exactly how Beech was killed?"

"We are waiting for the pathologist's report on the head. But the initial report says there is evidence of severe blunt-force trauma to the back of the skull."

Shocked though she was, Agatha was aware of a heavy atmosphere of suspicion in the room. I've got to solve this case, she thought wildly. I'm rapidly becoming the number one suspect. But that's ridiculous. I would hardly send a severed head to myself. And where is the rest of the body? The feet and legs are missing.

"Mrs. Raisin!" said Wilkes sharply. "Pay attention. I want you to go back to the late Mrs. Richards. We must assume that she knew something and that was the reason she was killed."

"You have my statement," said Agatha. "I

139

gave you everything then."

"Nonetheless. Go over it again."

Agatha eventually had to be supported from the interview room by a policewoman. She felt her legs had turned to jelly. James was waiting for her.

"I rescued your cats from the garden," he said, "and took them to my place. I suggest you move in with me until things are safer. It's all right, Officer, I'll take her home."

"Take me for a drink first," said Agatha.

"It's just a few minutes before eleven in the morning. Too early."

"James, I'm sure the sun is over the poop deck or whatever. I *need* a drink."

"Agatha, that is a warning sign. When people start saying they need a drink, they're on the slippery slope to alcoholism."

A fit of rage brought the strength back to Agatha's legs. "Goodbye," she said abruptly, and left police headquarters, banging the door noisily behind her.

She headed straight for the Dragon pub across the other side of the car park, deaf to the sound of James shouting something from behind her.

There was a light breeze. The pub had tables outside with large glass ashtrays on each one. "Civilisation at last," breathed Agatha.

She sat down, opened her handbag, took out her lighter and a packet of Bensons and lit a cigarette. A shadow fell across her.

"Gin and tonic?" asked James.

"Make it a double," said Agatha, squinting up at him out of her bearlike eyes.

When James went into the pub, Agatha pulled out her mobile and dialled Toni. "See if you can renew your friendship with Mrs. Richards," said Agatha after she had finished describing the horrors of the morning. "She might know something. I mean, this Richards character strikes me as fishy."

"Patrick did a check on him," said Toni cautiously. "He is what he appears to be — a successful businessman."

"Nonetheless, do it," said Agatha, "and I want Phil following behind you to keep a watch on you, just in case."

James came back as she rang off, carrying her drink and a coffee for himself. Agatha suddenly found herself missing Charles. She did not want to move in with James. She would not be allowed to smoke. And his fussy bachelor ways would get on her nerves. Her cottage was protected by first-class security.

"I think I'd be better off in my own

141

home," said Agatha after a gulp of her drink. "It is secure. Come on, James, you know we'd get on each other's nerves."

He gave a reluctant smile. In that moment, Agatha wavered. Oh, those blue eyes of his and that smile which lit up his whole face. That hard, muscular body . . .

She gave herself a mental slap.

For his part, James felt that old pull of attraction towards Agatha. Her hair was shining in the sunlight, and the colour had returned to her face.

"Can't you just for once leave this one to the police?" he asked.

"No, I can't," said Agatha. "I must get to the bottom of things. What knowledge did a common copper like Beech have that was worth a lot of money? That's what I would like to know. His macabre death was revenge, I think, but also a warning to anyone else."

"Leave it for now, anyway," said James. "Let me take you home."

Agatha wavered but realised she was still weak from shock. "All right," she said, finishing her drink. "But I don't think I'll go home yet. It will still be full of police. I'll book a room at the George Hotel after I buy myself some cheap clothes."

Sir Charles Fraith heard the news of the dead head delivered to Agatha on the car radio later the next morning. When he arrived at his Warwickshire mansion, he went straight to the kitchen where he kept the keys to Agatha's cottage. They were usually hanging on a board along with various other keys to the garage, the cellar and so on. But Agatha's keys were missing. He called to his manservant, Gustav, "Have you taken Mrs. Raisin's keys?"

"Wouldn't touch them," said Gustav, who disapproved of Agatha.

"Ask around. The village women were in to clean, weren't they? And ask my aunt."

He waited impatiently until Gustav returned. "Nothing," he said with gloomy relish.

"Check all the locks. Make sure no one could have broken in."

"You probably left them somewhere."

"Oh, just do what you're told for once in your miserable life."

Gustav eventually found there were faint scratches around the lock on the kitchen door.

"I'd better get to Agatha quickly," said

143

Charles. "She isn't answering her phone."

A call to Bill Wong elicited the fact that Agatha was staying at the George. Charles got into his car and set off for Mircester.

Toni decided that it would be a mistake to visit Mrs. Richards in her home. With Phil in his car parked behind her car a little way away from the Richardses' villa but with a clear view of the front, Toni settled down to wait.

The news of Gary Beech's head had been flashed on television. If Fiona Richards saw it and her ex-husband was implicated in any way, she might rush to him — always assuming she knew something.

The day was unusually warm. The sun beat down on Toni's little car. After an hour, Fiona Richards appeared. She was on her own. Fiona drove off at a sedate pace, and Toni with Phil behind followed her black BMW.

Then Fiona parked in the town square. Toni slid into a parking place a few places away and set out to follow on foot.

To Toni's dismay, she went into the George Hotel. Agatha had phoned again before Toni had left the office to say that she would be staying at the George.

She heard the receptionist say, "Good day,

Mrs. Richards. Your friend is waiting for you in the dining room."

Toni had forgotten to take any money out of the petty cash and hoped her own credit card would stand the strain of a lunch at the George. She turned and saw Phil hovering behind her. "She's gone in for lunch to meet someone," said Toni. "I'd better go into the dining room as well."

"Don't waste your money on an expensive meal," said the ever-practical Phil. "You can't get near her when she's with someone. Go into the dining room and get a look at whoever she is meeting and then join me in the café across the road. We can have a cheap snack and wait until she comes out."

"Good idea." Phil went off, and Toni made her way through to the dining room.

Mrs. Richards was talking to a man, and from his appearance, Toni guessed that the man was her ex-husband. Agatha's notes on the case included detailed descriptions of all the people she had come across.

She retreated and joined Phil, who was seated at an outside table at the café. "It looks as if she's with her ex-husband," said Toni. "I'll try to talk to her again when she's on her own. I mean, she was friendly enough before."

"I'll go and have a look," said Phil. "I

sneaked a photograph of him."

He had just gone when Toni's mobile phone rang. It was Charles. "Do you know if Agatha is at the George?" he demanded. "It looks as if someone's stolen my set of keys to her cottage."

"Yes, she's staying at the George," said Toni. "I hope you didn't have the code to the burglar alarm with the keys."

"Oh, God, it's pasted above the hook."

"Charles!"

"Got to go."

Agatha awoke and blinked groggily. Someone was hammering at her hotel room door. She heard Charles's voice shouting, "Agatha! Open up!"

She struggled out of bed, shouting back, "Give me a minute."

Her hair was all over the place, and her face looked tired and white. She gathered up the set of cheap clothes she had bought, unlocked the door and dived into the bathroom. "Take a seat," she called. "Getting dressed. What's up?"

"I'll tell you when you come out."

Charles opened the minibar and helped himself to a whisky.

Agatha quickly showered and put on underwear and the loose cotton dress she

146

had bought. She brushed her hair until it shone and carefully applied a layer of make-up with a hand made expert over the years.

When she emerged, she glared at the glass of whisky in Charles's hand, noticing from two small empty bottles that it was not his first.

"Oh, do make yourself at home," she said sarcastically. "Hear about the head?"

"Yes, frightful."

"Is that why you are here raiding the mini-bar?"

"Well, not exactly. It's like this . . ."

Agatha heard him out and then said, "I'll get on to the security firm and get them round tomorrow. I suppose the police will be at my cottage for most of today. I should charge you. I'll need to change all the locks and the burglar alarm."

She sat down suddenly on the bed. "I still feel shaky. I went straight to bed when I got here."

"You need lunch."

"Are you buying?"

"Of course," said Charles reluctantly.

They were about to enter the dining room when Agatha saw Fiona Richards and her husband.

147

She backed away. "Let's get out of here," she hissed. "The Richards female is in there with her husband. We'll have lunch somewhere else."

As they left the hotel, Agatha spotted Phil and Toni in the café opposite and went to join them.

"I thought I would wait until she leaves and see if I can have a word with her," said Toni.

"But get her on her own."

"I'll try."

"We're off for lunch," said Agatha, and added firmly, "Charles is buying."

Charles, predictably, led Agatha to the Dragon, where he knew the set pub meals were cheap at lunchtime.

Bill Wong was just finishing his lunch as they walked in. "I'm going back out to your cottage, Agatha," he said. "I want to see if they've found out anything."

"I hope I'll be able to go home tomorrow," said Agatha, sitting next to him. "Charles, get me a steak and chips and a half of lager."

As Charles's well-tailored back moved towards the bar, Agatha whispered, "You'll never guess what the silly ass has done." She told him about the missing keys.

"I know. He did phone us," said Bill

148

crossly. "Come over to headquarters after lunch. We'll need to send someone out to Warwickshire to have a look at that kitchen door."

Bill left them when their food arrived. Agatha poked dismally at her steak. When she was with James, she longed for Charles's lighter company. Now, she felt she could do with James's steady reassurance.

Her phone rang. It was Roy Silver, babbling with excitement. "I hear you've found the head."

"Well, it found me."

"Look, Aggie, how about me coming down for the week-end and babysitting you?"

"Yes, sure. Do you want me to pick you up at the station?"

"No, I'm driving down. See you Friday evening."

Toni at last saw the Richardses leaving the hotel. Tom Richards kissed his ex-wife on the cheek and strode off. Fiona Richards set off in the opposite direction. Toni had already paid the bill in the café, so she followed in pursuit, with Phil following a discreet distance behind.

Fiona went into a dress shop, and after only a little hesitation, Toni followed her in just as a formidable sales assistant was ushering Fiona into a changing room, saying, "I've got the very thing for you. Cerise silk." She swung a frumpy outfit off its hanger and handed it into the changing room.

Fiona Richards was a contrast to the dead Amy, thought Toni, patiently waiting for her to come out. Amy wouldn't have been seen dead in a frock like that.

"How much is that dress you have just given that lady to try on?" asked Toni.

"Four hundred and ninety-nine pounds."

"Bit steep."

The assistant looked coldly at Toni. "Do you want something?"

"I just want a word with Mrs. Richards."

The assistant went into the changing room. "What do you think?"

"May as well. I need something for the Woman of the Year banquet."

"Ooh, have you been selected?"

"Hardly. I'm just a housewife. Yes, I'll take it."

"There's a young lady waiting to speak to you."

Fiona glanced out of the changing room and then shut the door. "I do not wish to speak to her. Tell her to go away. She's one of those awful detectives."

The assistant approached Toni. "Come into my office, please. I want a word with you. Come along, or I'll call the police."

Once in the small office, which smelled of perfume and cloth, the assistant said, "Mrs. Richards doesn't want to speak to you, and she has made that perfectly clear. You will leave immediately."

At that moment, they both heard the shop door bang.

The assistant looked out of the window and saw Fiona scurrying off down the street. "You've lost me a sale," she wailed.

Toni ran out of the shop, looking to right and left, but could see no sign of Fiona.

Phil was remarkably spry for seventy-odd years. He followed Fiona to the car park. She had been moving very quickly, taking a circuitous route through market stalls to the car park.

She was just about to get into her car when Phil approached her. "Excuse me!"

Fiona surveyed him. Phil had white hair and a gentle face.

"What is it?"

"I think I saw a couple of youths trying to break into your car. They saw me and ran off. Maybe you'd better go to the police station and I'll help you put in a report."

151

"The police won't do anything," said Fiona. "Useless. But thanks all the same."

Phil gave a charming laugh. "I don't know what they would have done if they had confronted me. Bit long in the tooth. You know, you look a bit shaken. Fancy a cup of tea?" As she hesitated, he added, "With my years, you can hardly think I'm trying to pick you up."

"Oh, all right. I could do with a cuppa. I had lunch at the George and there was too much salt in the food."

"There's a new café just next to the abbey," said Phil.

"Lead the way."

Over a pot of tea and toasted tea cakes in a shady garden at the back of the café, Fiona visibly relaxed as Phil prattled on about the unseasonably warm weather.

"Are you originally from Mircester?" asked Phil.

"No, I'm a London girl. I think when the kids are old enough, I'll move back. Never really settled here."

"But the countryside is so beautiful!" exclaimed Phil.

"It's not even real countryside. Neat little fields. Manicured rubbish to keep rich farmers in their four-wheelers."

"I don't know that the farmers have all

that easy a time of it," ventured Phil. "I mean, they're so dependent on the weather."

"And government subsidies," said Fiona.

Phil decided to quickly abandon that subject.

"Are you married?" he realised Fiona was asking.

"No. Are you?"

"Was. But we have friendly relations because of the children. Do you know his wife was found murdered the other day?"

"Good heavens!" said Phil. "I read about a murder at Tesco's in Stow."

"That's the one."

"Why her? Is it because she was at one time married to that policeman who was murdered as well?"

"Probably. I don't know why she was murdered of all people. She was a silly, common little thing. My ex was married to her."

"No wonder you want to leave the countryside," exclaimed Phil. "You must be frightened to death."

"Why?"

"Some psycho is going around murdering people."

"Ah, but I didn't know the horrible Gary Beech."

"If you didn't know him, how do you know he was horrible?"

"His penchant for ticketing everyone was legendary. You do ask a lot of questions."

"Comes from being retired," said Phil. "I live a pretty lonely life, and I get curious about people. More tea?"

"No thanks. I'd better be getting home. Wolfgang's due back from school, and the younger ones are with the nanny."

"How old are they?"

"Wolfgang's thirteen, Josie's five and Carol is four. Carol goes to a kindergarten twice a week. That's all. She's not very strong."

"What's the matter with her?"

"Nobody knows. She seems to be physically healthy, but she cries a lot. Look, I've enjoyed talking to you. Give me your card. Maybe we'll meet up again."

"I'd like that." Phil carefully extracted a card that had only his home number and address.

"Carsely." Her eyes sharpened. "Now why does that ring a bell?"

"Been in the papers," said Phil easily. "That woman detective had a head delivered to her."

"God, how awful. Agatha Raisin, isn't it? Well, she's in a man's world, so she'll just have to learn to take it."

When she had left, Phil thoughtfully

154

ordered more tea and phoned Toni. "I'd leave her to me," he finished, then asked, "What happened in that shop?"

Toni told him. "Her ex-husband probably warned her off," said Phil. "I've established some sort of friendship. Why is Agatha so interested? Fiona seems an ordinary house-wife."

"Agatha is suspicious of Richards despite his clean bill of health from the police. She feels Fiona might know something without being aware of it. She feels there is some-thing seriously wrong with a man who wants women to go and get face-lifts."

Phil finally finished drinking his tea and made his way out. He had an odd feeling of being watched, so to be on the safe side, he did not go back to the office.

That evening, Agatha was settling down to a solitary meal at the George, wondering bitterly why James had not tried to contact her, when a tall, well-groomed man ap-proached her table. He was dressed in smart casual. He had silver hair and a tanned face, hooded pale eyes and a fleshy mouth.

"Mrs. Raisin?"

"Yes?" demanded Agatha suspiciously.

He slid into a chair opposite her. "My name is Guy Brandon. I'm the main judge in the Woman of the Year."

"I was very flattered to be nominated," said Agatha eagerly. "Have you eaten?"

"Yes, but I'll have a coffee and brandy if that's all right with you."

Agatha waved the waiter over and gave the order.

"I really think you should get the prize," he said. "You're quite a legend."

"Thank you."

"Oh, I'm behind you, but the other two judges, well, they favour Cressida Jones-Wilkes."

"Who the hell is she? Never heard of her."

"She runs a very successful garden centre on the Stow road."

His brandy and coffee arrived. "Of course, the other two judges could be made to change their minds. But it costs money."

Agatha opened her handbag and surreptitiously switched on a powerful little tape recorder. "Sorry," she said, "I was looking for my cigarettes. I always forget about the smoking ban. You were saying that the other two judges could be *bribed?*"

He threw his head back and laughed, displaying a mouthful of large, cosmetically whitened teeth.

"You have the reputation for being blunt, Mrs. Raisin. But just think of the boost it would give your detective agency if you were elected. Midlands television are going to cover the event."

"How much?" demanded Agatha.

"I should think two thousand pounds each should settle the matter."

"Who are the other two judges?"

"Mary Mamble, who runs the Arts Centre, and Sir Jonathan Beery."

"You used to be an MP, didn't you?" asked Agatha. "You lost your seat at the last election. What are you doing now?"

"This and that. I write articles for the papers and sit on several committees. I am much in demand. In fact, I am a pretty famous public speaker."

"I am not going to hand out money until I know I am elected," said Agatha. "Tell them that as soon as I am, they will get the money."

"And two thousand to me," said Guy quickly. "I have to do all the work of persuading them."

"All right," said Agatha. "Same deal. I get elected and you and the others get paid immediately afterwards. I assume you all want cash?"

"You are so quick on the uptake."

"Amn't I just," said Agatha, her bearlike eyes glinting oddly in the light. "But get this. This is a ladies' agreement. You do not see any cash until the deed is done."

"But surely . . . I mean, a little in advance?"

"Not a penny."

"I suppose I'll have to trust you."

"Oh, you'd better. For your own good."

"I'll be in touch." He smoothed back his hair with a nervous hand.

Oh, dear, thought Agatha, watching his retreating back. What a wicked world!

Chapter Eight

Roy Silver drove happily down into Carsely early on Friday evening. He wondered whether Agatha would admire his new appearance. His hair had started to grow again, so he had gelled it into spikes. Very much taken with his punk appearance, he had decided to go for the retro look and was wearing flares and an open-necked shirt, displaying a gold medallion on his skinny, hairless chest.

He parked behind Agatha's car and got out. He was opening the boot to take out his small suitcase when he was seized from behind and something cold and hard was thrust against his neck.

"One squeak out of you and you're dead," growled a voice.

Terrified, Roy felt himself being dragged into a van and thrown in the back. The van took off with a roar. Where was Agatha? wondered Roy, trembling uncontrollably. A man wearing a balaclava sat in the back of the van, holding a gun on him. He searched Roy's pockets and took away his wallet and mobile phone.

"Why are you doing this?" pleaded Roy.

"If the Raisin woman does as she's told, then you've nothing to fear," said the man. "So shut up and stop whimpering or I will shoot you."

As the evening dragged on without any sign of Roy, Agatha tried his mobile phone but did not get any reply. Then there was a ring at the doorbell. Roy, at last. She opened it and found James on the doorstep.

"I thought you were Roy," said Agatha. "I'm expecting him."

"His car's parked outside. Maybe he's gone for a walk round the village, although it looks as if a storm is coming."

Agatha felt fear clutch at her heart. "But he wouldn't go for a walk after a long drive from London. Oh, God, what if something's happened to him?"

"Calm down. What could anyone want with Roy?"

"Blackmail," whispered Agatha. "They tried to frighten me off with that head."

"I never saw anything. I've only just got home."

Agatha took a deep breath. "I'm calling the police."

Roy was taken out of the van and thrust into a half-derelict cottage. At gunpoint, he was shoved into a small room and the door was shut and locked behind him.

He looked around wildly. There came a great crack of thunder, and then a flash of lightning lit up the room. He caught a glimpse of a mattress on the floor and a bucket in the corner. The window was barred.

He sank down into the floor and burst into tears.

The police refused to let Agatha go out hunting for Roy. They said it would be better if she stayed by the phone in case there was a ransom demand. Toni, Phil and Patrick all set off in their cars to scour the countryside.

Roy had been taken at dinnertime — teatime for the elderly residents — and everyone in the village had been indoors, or that was the way it seemed, because the police received the same reply as they went from door to door — no one had seen anything.

Roy scrubbed his eyes dry with the sleeve

of his shirt as the cottage seemed to rock under the ferocity of the storm breaking overhead.

In all his misery and fear, there was one little nugget of comfort — he had not fouled himself. He had read in books that people did that under duress.

He tried to be calm and search the room for any possible means of escape, but his legs were trembling too much and he sat down on the floor and began to sob. He had never believed in God, had been almost proud of the fact, but now, in extremis, he prayed for deliverance as he had never prayed before as the storm roared in ferocity.

Then, as his sobbing subsided, he suddenly felt exhausted and weary.

His eyes were just closing as he sat with his back to the wall when there was a tremendous explosion. He was to find out later that a thunderbolt had hit the roof. The door to his room was blown open as if by dynamite.

He staggered to his feet, his only thought one of escape. He no longer cared if his captors were lurking around. He ran through a wrecked, smouldering kitchen and out into the driving rain.

Roy looked around wildly. A jagged flash

of lightning lit up his surroundings. Nothing but fields on either side. But far in the distance, he could see headlights of cars on a road.

He half ran, half stumbled, across fields, soaked to the skin, as the thunder rumbled off in the distance, and on the horizon, he could see one small pale star in the sky.

He finally reached the main road and stood waving his arms frantically at cars. He looked a weird figure, and at first, it seemed as if no one was going to stop. At last a small Volkswagen pulled up. A man in a dog collar got out and asked, "Are you in trouble?"

"Take me to the nearest police station," begged Roy.

Agatha sat by the phone in her cottage. Her friend Mrs. Bloxby held her hand. Equipment had been set up to record any calls. Two men crouched over it. Alice Peterson, the pretty detective constable, was making another pot of tea.

"I'll never forgive myself," said Agatha for the umpteenth time. "The whole horror of finding that head is beginning to get to me. I should never have let Roy come on a visit."

"You weren't to know. Where is Mr. Lacey?"

"Out searching for Roy."

"And Sir Charles?"

"Haven't even tried to reach him. I'll put on the television." There was a small set on the kitchen counter.

Agatha switched it on to BBC 24 Hour News. Alice said, "If he had been found, he would have phoned you."

"Not if it's his dead body that's been found," said Agatha.

The evening dragged on into the early hours of the morning. Agatha fell asleep with her head on the table. Mrs. Bloxby quietly left.

Alice, seated on a chair next to Agatha, felt her eyes begin to close. Suddenly, the voice of the news presenter crashed into her thoughts: "Breaking news. Public relations officer Roy Silver, friend of detective Agatha Raisin, who claims he was kidnapped, is at Chipping Norton Police Station, and we are just awaiting his comments."

"Wake up!" cried Alice, shaking Agatha.

"What?"

"Roy's been found. He's in Chipping Norton Police Station and about to emerge and make a statement."

The camera showed the outside of the police station, where a large number of press and television reporters and cameramen were gathered.

"The bastard!" hissed Agatha. "Do you know what he's done? Somehow he got free and got help, and instead of phoning me or the police at Mircester, he must have got hold of someone's phone and called Associated Press and every television company he could think of. I'd better phone Mrs. Bloxby. No, on second thought better not. The vicar would be furious if I woke them up in the middle of the night for any reason."

"Would you like to go over to Chipping Norton?"

"No," said Agatha grumpily. "I'm going to bed."

Roy had forgotten about the miracle of his deliverance. He was addicted to appearing on television.

He had begged the vicar for use of his mobile "to phone his mother." Roy's mother had died when he was still a child. Clutching the phone, and as soon as he was in the police station, Roy begged to use the lavatory, and once in there, he began assiduously to phone the press.

He then emerged, thanked the vicar, handed over the mobile and was examined by a police doctor before the questioning began. To his fury, after only half an hour, he was rushed out of the back of the police station and into a waiting car to take him to Mircester. Frantic, Roy could see his moment of fame slipping away.

He tried to reassure himself with the thought that the press would no doubt guess where he had gone. But to his dismay, he was taken to a safe house, told to rest and put under guard.

For the first time, he thought of Agatha and realised how furious she would be. He slept uneasily and woke in the morning to the sound of a policeman delivering his overnight bag. "May I use the phone?" asked Roy.

"No, you may not," said the policeman heavily. "The vicar, Mr. Prentice, who rescued you, checked his mobile and found you had made ten phone calls, most of them to London. He will send you a bill."

Roy flushed miserably. He dressed and was served two soggy croissants and a cup of instant coffee before being taken off to police headquarters to endure hours of questioning.

He had planned to give a highly embroidered account, but faced with Wilkes's severe face and Bill Wong's admonitory stare, he told nothing but the truth. He omitted only his frantic prayer. In the light of day, praying to God seemed such a wimpish thing to have done. I don't want to lose my street cred, thought Roy.

At last the questioning was over. Now to face the cameras, thought Roy. But he waited over an hour before being hustled out of a back door where Alice was waiting to drive him to Carsely.

"The press are following us," said Alice. "Do you want me to shake them off?"

"No, no!" screeched Roy. "I can handle them."

To his delight, just after Alice drove off after leaving him outside Agatha's cottage, he saw the vanguard of the press arrive. He had changed into jeans and a T-shirt because his retro clothes were a wreck.

He was standing on Agatha's doorstep, clearing his throat and waiting for his big moment to begin, when the door behind him opened and Agatha Raisin said, "You horrible little man," in a loud, clear voice.

"But Aggie," pleaded Roy, "I've been kidnapped and could have been murdered."

James appeared behind Agatha and drew her back into the house. "He's been through a lot. Let him have his bit of fame."

Roy rallied but gave a plainer statement than he would have otherwise done and

167

therefore a more impressive one.

When he finally joined Agatha and James in the kitchen, it was to find Mrs. Bloxby there as well.

Agatha gave him a cup of coffee. They had heard his story through the open front door.

"That was a miraculous thing to happen," exclaimed Agatha. "I mean that thunder-bolt."

Roy glanced at Mrs. Bloxby and blushed to the roots of his newly gelled hair. To Alice's annoyance, Roy had insisted on stopping at a chemist's on the road to Carsely to buy an extra tub of gel and then had gone through contortions in the front seat of the police car, trying to peer in the driving mirror.

"Why are you blushing?" demanded Agatha suspiciously.

"It must really have been a divine deliverance," said Mrs. Bloxby gently. "Were you praying, Roy?"

"Ever so hard," said Roy, and began to sob, dry sobs like a child who has nearly cried itself out.

"There, now," said Agatha, visibly softening towards him. "I think it would be best if you had something to eat and a lie-down. Phone your boss and say you won't be in on Monday."

"What if they come for me again?" asked Roy.

"You come to the vicarage with me," said Mrs. Bloxby. "I won't tell anyone except the police where you are."

Roy meekly and gratefully allowed himself to be led away.

Agatha and James were joined by Bill Wong and Alice just after Roy had left. Agatha told them that Roy was at the vicarage.

When they were all seated round the table, Bill began. "This is obviously not the work of some lone psycho. It's not someone who thought they got a parking ticket too many. This looks like a gang, and that usually means drugs or prostitution.

"But there has been no evidence of drug dealing on a large scale in Mircester, or of any prostitution ring. What use could a market town copper like Gary Beech be to a criminal gang? It must be something so good and so profitable that they have been driven to murder, intimidation and kidnap."

"Terrorism?" suggested James.

"The intelligence services have not found anything."

"That doesn't mean to say it doesn't exist," Agatha pointed out. "But, say these people were terrorists. What good would Beech have been to them?"

"He was always ferreting around," said Bill. "He could have discovered enough to blackmail them."

"But," protested James, "why, with Beech out of the way, still go after Agatha? Maybe they thought Roy was her son."

Agatha bridled. She hated to be reminded of her age.

"The thing is," said Bill slowly, "you are all at risk: you, Agatha, James and your staff. In the past there has been a lot in the media about your successes, Agatha. They want to make sure you don't find out anything."

"Was there any clue in that —" Agatha coloured and bit her lip. She had been about to ask if the ledger found in Beech's secret room had given them any clues.

"In what?" demanded Bill suspiciously.

"In, for example, the cottage to which Roy was taken. Who does it belong to?"

"It's a derelict building out in the fields of a farm that's been on the market for the past six months. The farmer is in an old folks' home, and his heirs don't want to continue with the farm and so no one lives there. No fingerprints. The storm scrubbed everything pretty clean when part of the roof caved in. By the way, that vicar who gave Roy a lift to Chipping Norton Police

Station would like to be paid for the phone calls."

"Which calls?" asked Agatha.

"Roy asked if he could borrow the man's mobile to call his mother."

"She's dead!"

"Anyway, he used it to phone a lot of the media."

Agatha sighed. "I'll make sure Roy pays him back." She suddenly felt low as she looked at Bill's pleasant face. Bill was the only normal man she knew. James was a cold fish, Charles was flighty, and Roy, a publicity-grabbing pain in the fundament. At that moment, Bill exchanged a smile with pretty Alice, and Agatha felt a stabbing pang of jealousy.

"Now," said Bill. "We will put a guard on your cottage and one on your office. But we cannot guard the homes of all of your staff. For your own safety, you should close your business, let everyone go off somewhere safe and leave the detection to the police."

"In the middle of a recession!" exclaimed Agatha.

"You would not like anything to happen to Toni, for example," said Bill. "I want you to announce in the press that you are dropping all your investigations into this case to protect your staff. At least will you do that?"

Their conversation had been periodically interrupted by rings at the doorbell. "The press are still outside, Agatha. Go and do it now."

"Oh, all right," said Agatha. "I must admit, whoever they are, they've really got me scared."

They waited while she made her statement.

She eventually returned in a bad temper. The press had seen her capitulation as possibly the end to more horror stories and had tried to goad her about "giving in."

After Bill and Alice had left, James stayed on guard with Agatha, pointing out that she was at risk until her story appeared in the news. Agatha was waiting for workmen to come and beef up her security, change the locks and change the burglar alarm code and for a local man to put bars on all the downstairs windows.

James made an omelette for lunch and then waited with Agatha until the workmen had finished.

"I think you should move in with me," he said again.

Agatha gave a reluctant smile. "May I smoke?"

"No."

"Then no thanks. But thanks all the same for sticking by me and looking after my cats. I'll go to the office now, and tell everyone to leave the investigation into Beech's death alone."

"Including you?"

"Yes, including me," said Agatha.

Everything seemed to go very quiet in Agatha's life after her statement appeared on television and in the press.

May came in, cold, blustery and rainy, but then cleared up into long, sunny days.

Agatha had prepared herself carefully for the Woman of the Year banquet. Her favourite hairdresser, Jeanelle, had recoloured her hair to a rich, glossy brown, and her beautician, Dawn, had performed a series of nonsurgical face-lifts. Agatha felt ready for what she privately considered the battle ahead.

Wearing a soft white chiffon blouse, her good pearls and a black silk chiffon skirt with a slit up the side and high heels, Agatha drove to the George Hotel, looking always in her driving mirror to check any cars behind her that might look suspicious. She had not lost her fear of the murderers of Gary Beech.

The restaurant, which had been taken over

for the evening for the event, was already crowded when she arrived. She was directed to a table that held three other nominees: Cressida Jones-Wilkes, the woman who owned a nursery; Joanna Tripp, local poetess, and Fairy Mather, a stocky woman who painted angry abstracts.

"You're that detective woman who chickened out of a case out of fear," said Fairy truculently.

Agatha's small eyes narrowed. "What were your parents thinking of to give you a name like Fairy?" she said. "You look more like a troll."

"Why, you bitch!"

"Yes, that's me. Pass the wine."

The three contestants looked uneasily at Agatha.

"I have never been so insulted in my life," said Fairy at last.

"Time you were, then," said Agatha. "Oh, snakes and bastards, mulligatawny soup, and on such a hot evening. Couldn't they do better than that?"

Joanna Tripp, neat in a pink blouse and evening skirt, small features and heavy glasses, looked at Agatha with disgust. "You are a truly horrible woman," she remarked.

Joanna wrote "sweet" poems about the Cotswolds in the local magazines and newspapers. Even to Agatha's half-educated mind, they seemed like doggerel.

She surveyed the poetess and said, "Why don't you shut up and go away / And live to fight another day."

The three women moved their chairs closer together as if for comfort and began to talk to one another in low whispers.

The soup was followed by a plate of chicken and mashed potatoes in a gummy white sauce. The George was usually famous for its food. As that course was followed by a sliver of cheesecake, Agatha reflected that it was the most cut-price meal she had ever endured.

As the coffee was served, Guy Brandon took the microphone. Most of the men at the banquet were wearing black tie, but Guy was wearing a pale blue sweater over a striped shirt and very tight jeans.

He began to "amuse." He twittered, he clowned, he laughed hilariously at his own jokes, and in all, thought Agatha, he bored for Britain.

The evening wore on. Guy had a very loud voice. There was a speaker right over Agatha's table, and she began to feel that endless voice was booming inside her head. People began to shift restlessly, and the laughter grew thin and sporadic. Only the other three contestants at last were left to laugh sycophantically at each new sally.

At last, the mayor, seated behind Guy on the stage, leaned forward and tapped his watch.

"Ah, yes . . ." Guy beamed. "The great moment. If you will just pass me that envelope, Mayor. Who have we here?" He grinned at the audience. "And the winner is . . ." Long silence.

Someone shouted, "Oh, get on with it!"

Guy scowled. "The winner is . . . Mrs. Agatha Raisin! Come on up, Mrs. Raisin!" he cried.

Cameras flashed as Agatha made her way to the little stage. Guy flung an arm around her shoulders. "What have you got to say? You must be overwhelmed."

"I have to say this," said Agatha, seizing the microphone. "I am sure you would all like to know how the judging is done. Listen to this." She held a tape recorder up to the microphone and switched it on. The whole room could clearly hear Guy suggesting she pay him and the other judges for the prize.

When the recording had finished, Guy began to back off the stage, and a chorus of jeers and catcalls rang in his ears. The newspaper reporters were furious because all this was too late for the morning editions and television would scoop the lot. But each reporter decided to do a really nasty piece on Guy for the day afterwards.

Agatha raised her hands for silence. "In view of this chicanery," she said, "I think the prize should be divided up amongst the three other nominees and that each of them should be given the title of Woman of the Year. Come along, girls."

Guy fled. The three women who had spent the evening loathing Agatha all now joined her with beaming smiles.

Bill Wong, watching local television news before he went to work, stared at the screen in a mixture of anger and dismay. Didn't Agatha know that it was important these days to keep a low profile? Guy Brandon was interviewed. He said it had all been a bit of a joke that Mrs. Raisin had taken seriously. She had a reputation as being a pushy and ambitious woman, and he had just wondered how far she would go. The interviewer then demanded why he had gone ahead and elected her. He hummed and hawed and mumbled something and then fled the studio after unplugging his microphone.

Agatha found Bill waiting for her as she opened up her office. She had never seen the usually placid detective so angry.

"How could you?" he raged. "The minute you had that tape you should have come to us. This is not the time to have a high profile. You're as bad as Roy. Grabbing publicity no matter what. You are a very silly woman."

"It was nothing to do with the case," howled Agatha defiantly. "Anyway, I'll bet you're no further forward in finding who murdered either Gary Beech or his ex-wife."

"We're pursuing certain leads," said Bill.

"Oh, yeah? Well, that means you've got zilch. I watch these real-life forensic programmes on TV and they always seem to find someone through a bit of hair or dust."

"If you were watching properly, you might have noticed that some of them take years to solve. Just be careful," he said in a quieter voice.

When he had left, Agatha sat down suddenly. The fear of whoever it was who had sent her that head two months ago had never gone away. She had a craving for sleep most days. She often thought during the day of the moment when she could get home and pull the duvet up round her ears. Death by duvet.

The fear ebbed as her temper rose. She

must find out something, anything, to try to break the case. She could not go on living like this.

Agatha looked up as her staff filed in. They discussed jobs to be covered that day.

"Aren't we ever going to find out what happened to Beech?" asked Toni.

"No," said Agatha sharply. "We will drop that one. Leave it to the police."

"When did we ever leave anything to the police?" said Patrick plaintively, but Agatha ignored him.

"And what are you doing today?" asked Phil after they all had their assignments.

"I've got paperwork to do," said Agatha. "Off you go."

She cast a quick suspicious glance at Toni as the girl left. Toni appeared to be carrying a golden glow around with her. I hope she's not found another unsuitable older man, thought Agatha.

Toni's job was to find a missing teenager. She had not told Agatha that she had found the girl the night before and had returned her to her parents. She needed the day free to meet Simon. They had arranged to meet in a teashop in Winter Parva, the one place Toni was sure Agatha would not visit. Simon had got in touch with her as soon as he had returned from Afghanistan on leave.

He had told her his impending wedding had all been a mistake. Susie, his intended, had turned out to be bossy. He had phoned Toni the night before to arrange to meet her, where he said he would explain everything.

As Toni parked near the teashop, Winter Parva was not living up to its name. Great fluffy clouds sailed in the blue sky above, and the trees in the main street were ruffled by the lightest of breezes. The old village cottages and shops lining the main street appeared to crouch beside the road like very old villagers surveying the passing of time. In these days of chain shops, Winter Parva had retained its individuality. There were teashops, souvenir shops, an ironmonger, a baker, a fishmonger and a butcher — all the traditional fabric of a Cotswold village. There was a huge church at one end, built by rich merchants in the days when the wool trade was at its height. Its huge Gothic spire cast a long finger of shadow down the main street like the pointer on a giant sundial.

Toni's heart rose as she saw Simon seated at a table in the bay window of the teashop. She recognised his thick hair and his jester's face.

When she joined him, they began to talk at once about the perfidy of Agatha Raisin,

180

until Toni said sadly, "You can hardly back out of the wedding now."

He hung his head and mumbled, "It's all got out of hand. The regiment's on leave and they're all going to be there. It's going to be a big production. Toni, the mayor is going to attend. I'm trapped. It's all Agatha's fault."

"Hardly," said Toni. "*She* wasn't in Afghanistan. *She* didn't make you propose to Susie."

"No, but I was feeling flat, and Susie's a good sort. She was very sympathetic, and one thing led to another."

"There's still time to get out of it," urged Toni. "Think of the misery of a loveless marriage."

"Oh, Susie does love me. Oh, what is it?"

"The waitress wants your order," said Toni.

They both ordered tea and scones. The shadow of the church spire moved across the window of the tearoom. Toni felt bleak. When Simon had phoned her, she was sure he was going to tell her the marriage was off.

"So you are going ahead with it," she said in a small voice.

"I have to —" Simon broke off as tea and scones arrived.

Toni gave a little sigh. "It's up to you. Why did you let it get so far?"

"She's pregnant."

"Oh, Simon!"

He shrugged. "Maybe being a dad will have a lot of compensations." He looked at her eagerly. "We can still see each other."

"No, we can't," said Toni roundly. "I've got my own life to lead, and creeping around meeting a married man doesn't come into it."

There was a long, awkward silence. Then Simon said, "Tell me about this dead policeman case."

Toni gave him a précis. "It sounds like a gang," she concluded. "Look at all the criminal gangs Britain let in after the European Union opened the borders: Bulgarians, Romanians and so on."

"But what is there for them in Mircester, of all places?" said Simon. "It's hardly a big city like Birmingham. For one thing, there's nowhere really to hide out. And is this Tom Richards squeaky clean? Seem a bit of an odd fish wanting two women to have plastic surgery."

"It's not as odd as you think. The divorce cases we handle are usually instigated by the women. The husband sees all these sexual fantasies on television and wants to try some of them out at home. The woman says no. Fights ensue. Divorce follows. I suppose wanting the wife to have plastic surgery is another part of the fantasy. Agatha's told us not to go near anything to do with the murders."

"Not like her."

"Well, getting a dead head through the post was enough to frighten even Agatha Raisin. I'd better be getting back, Simon. I won't be seeing you again."

"You'll come to my wedding?"

"No thanks."

"But I've invited the whole agency. They're all coming."

"Well, in that case, I might drop along."

CHAPTER NINE

When Toni reached her car, she had a sudden urge to watch Mrs. Fiona Richards. Phil had told her that Fiona had not called him, and when he had called her, she'd said she was too busy. Amy Richards might have said something to her husband, and he might have told Fiona. It might be he was too afraid to pass any information along to the police in case something happened to him. In her car, she put on a baseball cap and pulled it down over her face and put on a pair of dark glasses. Satisfied she looked like any other anonymous teenager, she set out for Fiona Richards's house. Fiona's car was not in the drive.

Toni set off for the centre of town. Perhaps Fiona had gone to do some shopping. It was market day. Toni walked up and down between the stalls. As lunchtime approached, she decided to try the George. She checked the hotel's private parking place and recognised Fiona's car. Toni decided to sit in an armchair in reception and say she was waiting for someone.

Armed with a newspaper, she glanced round it occasionally as people entered the hotel.

She found to her surprise as she waited that she no longer felt anything for Simon at all. He had only been a dream. If Agatha had not interfered, then the dream would not have been kept alive.

"Excuse me, are you Toni Gilmour?"

Toni lowered her newspaper. A man was standing there, smiling down at her. She registered that he was very expensively dressed and immaculately barbered. He smelled faintly of cologne. He had a wide, pleasant face, and although his body was broad, it looked sturdy. His eyes were brown with little flecks of gold.

"I am Toni Gilmour," said Toni, thinking her baseball cap and dark glasses had turned out to be a pretty poor disguise.

He sat down beside her. "It's cheeky of me to come right up to you. I wanted your advice. It's really Mrs. Raisin I want to meet. Here's my card. I'm Peter Powell, estate agent."

"And what did you want with Mrs. Raisin?" asked Toni suspiciously.

185

"It's like this. I've got this client who wants a cottage in the Cotswolds. He was driving with me around the villages and we ended up in Carsely. He fell in love with Mrs. Raisin's cottage."

"Odd that he should spot it," said Toni suspiciously. "It's in a cul-de-sac."

"He spotted it from the end of Lilac Lane. We drove up. He said he must have it."

"Agatha won't sell, I can tell you that."

"Ah, but wait to hear what he's offering."

"Who is this man?"

"At the moment he prefers to remain anonymous."

"Mr. . . ."

"Peter. Call me Peter."

"Peter, then. Agatha Raisin is a detective who has, until recently, been involved in two grizzly murders. She is going to be highly suspicious, as I am, of this mysterious buyer. In fact, I am going to have to report your interest to the police."

"You can check up on me anytime. I'm well-known in the real estate business. I have a good reputation."

"I think, then, they will be more interested in your client. Look at it this way. A prospective buyer would expect access to the house, would he not?"

"Well, of course."

"So the police will naturally want to know who and why."

"That's understandable. Go ahead."

After he had left, Toni crossed the hotel lobby and took a quick look inside the dining room. There was no sign of Fiona. She boldly asked at the desk whether a Mrs. Fiona Richards was in the hotel and learned to her dismay that she had left.

It must have happened while I was talking to that estate agent, thought Toni. I'm suspicious of everyone and everything. Does this estate agent really exist?

She was just crossing the square to police headquarters when she saw Bill Wong about to get into his car and hailed him. Toni decided it would be better to say nothing about watching Fiona, as they had all been warned off.

She told him about the estate agent and the prospective client for Agatha's cottage.

"I'd better look into it," said Bill. "Leave it with me. I mean, why did this estate agent approach you? Why not phone Agatha?"

Toni then phoned Agatha on her mobile and gave her a report. "Where were you when this man accosted you?" asked Agatha.

"I didn't tell Bill, but I happened to see

Fiona's car parked at the George, so I waited in reception. Then this estate agent distracted me, and after he had gone, so had she."

Agatha's voice was sharp with anxiety. "Toni, you are not to have anything to do with the murders. It's too dangerous. You've got that divorce case. Get on with it."

After Toni had left, Bill went back into the police station and typed out a short report on the estate agent and handed it to Wilkes.

"I see his firm is Powell, Slerry and Card," said Wilkes. "I've seen their FOR SALE boards. Get round there and have a word with him and insist on getting the name of his client."

The estate agent's offices were situated in the Glebe, one of the twisting mediaeval lanes around the abbey. He went in and asked for Mr. Powell. A girl disappeared into a back office and then indicated that he should go in. Powell rose from behind his desk and extended a large hand.

"Why am I being honoured with a visit from the police?" he asked.

"We are interested in your client who wishes to buy Agatha Raisin's cottage. May I have his name, please?"

"We do not give out names unless authorised to do so," said Powell.

"Oh, do be sensible," said Bill. "Do you want me to get a warrant and have your files thoroughly searched?"

"Would you mind stepping outside while I phone him? Just a courtesy to a client."

Bill waited impatiently, knowing he had little chance of getting a warrant without having any solid proof of criminal activity.

Powell came out of his office and handed him a slip of paper. "His name is Bogdan Staikov. You'll find him at the George right now."

"What nationality?"

Powell smiled. "You'll need to ask him."

At the George, Bill was told that Mr. Staikov was taking coffee on the terrace.

He walked through the hotel and onto the terrace overlooking the gardens at the back. He had not asked to be conducted to Staikov, feeling sure he would spot the foreigner right away. But there were a good few smokers enjoying their after-lunch coffees, and they all looked very British.

As he hesitated in the doorway, a small, silver-haired man got to his feet and waved him over. "Mr. Powell said you would be looking for me," he said. He had a slight trace of accent. His eyes, like Bill's were slightly elongated, but as grey and cold as the North Sea. He was wearing a lightweight cream-coloured suit with a blue shirt and striped silk tie. He had thick grey skin, a small mouth and nose and odd pointed ears.

"Please sit down," he said. "Coffee?"

"No, thank you. Why are you interested in Mrs. Raisin's cottage?"

"What are you talking about? I have been looking at many properties."

"Mrs. Raisin's cottage is in Lilac Lane in Carsely."

"Ah, yes, Carsely. I liked it. I want a new home for my daughter. So typically English. What has this to do with the police?"

Bill told him.

Staikov raised well-manicured hands in dismay. "I did not know. I do not read the newspapers. I am retired. My son now runs the business. I wish the quiet English life."

"What is your nationality?" asked Bill.

"I am originally from Bulgaria, but I married a British woman and settled here some twenty years ago."

"What was your business?"

"Clothing. Suede, leather, that sort of thing. My son now runs the business. Country Fashions. Our place is out in the industrial estate."

"Would you mind if I had a look around

your premises?"

He shrugged. "Go ahead. You British have only to hear the word *Bulgarian* and you think Mafia."

Toni had waited until Bill had left police headquarters and followed him to the estate agent's and then to the George. Once again, she went into the George. The restaurant was now empty apart from one couple, but she heard the sound of voices from the terrace, approached it and had a quick look, where she saw Bill talking to a silver-haired man.

Toni found a seat in the reception area, half-shielded by a cheese plant, and waited. Bill was not very long. After ten minutes, the man he had been talking to went out. Toni followed. He got into a chauffeur-driven Mercedes. Toni wished she had brought her car.

She approached the desk. She was just wondering whether to pose as a reporter when the receptionist said, "What can I do for you, Miss Gilmour?"

Toni cursed Agatha's penchant for getting their photos in the newspapers and on television. "I just wondered about the identity of that gentleman who just left?"

"Oh, that would be Mr. Staikov."

"Film business?"

"No, clothing business."

The receptionist turned away to deal with someone else. Toni made her way to the offices of the *Mircester Mercury,* where she knew an old school friend, John Worthing, had a job as a reporter.

John was delighted to see her. He was an owlish young man with limp brown hair. He had been bullied at school until he had come under the protection of the tough and popular Toni.

"I haven't seen you in ages," he said. "Anytime there's a story about you, the chief reporter gets it."

"I'm here to ask a favour."

"Anything."

"Could you look up a man called Staikov in your files?"

"Sure. Hasn't your voice got posh!"

"It's not posh. It's neutral," said Toni. "Be a love and get cracking."

"Wait till I heat up the computer."

"You are on broadband, aren't you?"

"Mircester Broadband."

Toni grinned in sympathy. Mircester Internet connection was rumoured to be the slowest in Gloucestershire.

At last he gave a grunt of triumph. "Here he is. We did a story when he retired last year. He has a clothing business out on the industrial estate. Originally from Bulgaria. Imports leather mostly. Rags-to-riches story. Arrived here pretty broke and made a fortune."

"I wonder how he got British nationality?"

"Married an English local. She died four years ago."

"What did she die of?"

"Hang on." John clicked away. "Ah, here we are. Fell down a flight of stairs."

"Did she now," remarked Toni, feeling a stir of excitement. "Got a report of the inquest?"

"Here we go. Verdict, accident. Pathologist said she was as drunk as a skunk."

"What's the name of this clothing firm?" asked Toni.

"Country Fashions."

"Thanks a lot."

"Toni, wait a minute. Do you think we might meet up one evening?"

He looked at her with pleading eyes, and Toni suddenly remembered a younger John, crying in the corner of the playground.

"I'm pretty busy," she said diplomatically. But as his face fell, she said quickly, "I tell you what I'll do for you. Give me your card, and if I've got a big story, you'll be the first to know."

"That would be great. I mean, everyone's out on some story or another and I'm left here to edit the letters page."

Outside, Toni phoned Agatha, who said quickly, "I'm in the office. Get round here. I want to hear every bit of it."

When Toni finished her report, Agatha's eyes shone with excitement. "I knew there must be some gang behind it. Must be the Mafia. I'd like to get inside that factory."

"I should think that's impossible," said Toni. "Anyway, I'm sure that's the first thing Bill would have done."

Patrick Mulligan walked in at that moment. Agatha rapidly told him what Toni had found out.

Tall and lugubrious and with the shiniest shoes in Mircester, Patrick looked every bit the retired policeman.

When Agatha had finished, he said, "There's a café out on the estate. Well, it's just a shack with tables outside. I'll get out there and see if I can meet any of the workers."

When Patrick had left, Toni said uneasily, "We weren't going to investigate the murders. Isn't this a bit dangerous?"

"Not unless this Bulgarian has anything

to do with it," said Agatha. "Don't you see? I've decided we're always going to be in danger if we don't solve these murders."

Before he went to the industrial estate, Patrick went home and changed out of his suit collar and tie and shiny shoes. He put on old casual clothes, a scuffed pair of boat shoes and a baseball cap.

It was a glorious day in June. He cycled out to the estate, feeling he needed the exercise. The English are not very used to good summers, and the warm weather appeared to have taken a lot of people by surprise. He could see men and women carrying coats and jackets.

He cycled into the industrial estate and propped his bicycle at the side of the café. He realised he hadn't had any lunch and ordered a hamburger, chips and tea. He could hear the man and woman who ran the café chattering in Polish. There were Poles everywhere in Gloucestershire. The lunch rush was over. He selected a table where he could get a good look at the entrance to Country Fashions.

Then he saw Bill Wong and Alice Peterson emerging and getting into their unmarked police car and driving off. He jerked down the peak of his baseball cap and turned his face away as the car slowed down opposite the café and then heaved a sigh of relief as it accelerated and drove off. He was served his hamburger, chips and tea. The tea was hot and freshly made. The hamburger was good, and to his amazement, the chips were from real potatoes, not the frozen kind.

He had a sudden longing to be able to sit here, relaxing in the sun, forgetting about detective work. But what would he do if he retired? He did not have any hobbies. Perhaps he and Phil could retire together and take up golf. At last, he decided reluctantly that he'd better get on with it and have a closer look at the factory.

As he approached it, a truck drove up and went round the back of the factory. Patrick paid for his food and pushed his bike in the direction the truck had gone. Men were unloading skins from the back of the truck.

"What are you doing here?" demanded a sharp voice.

Patrick swung round and found himself confronted by a man in the uniform of a security guard. Fortunately, Patrick had studied the list of businesses on a board as he had entered the industrial park.

"I think I'm lost," he said. "I need a pump for the pond in my garden."

"You want Aquaria Plus, Lot eleven, over

there," said the guard. Patrick got on his bicycle and cycled off.

Patrick lived in a flat and didn't have a garden, but he was always cautious, and some instinct prompted him to cycle to Aquaria Plus, dismount and go inside. As he inspected a selection of pumps, he glanced out of the window. The security guard was standing there. Patrick fell into conversation with a sales assistant, and when he looked up again, the security guard had gone. He waited a few minutes and then said apologetically that he would need to consult "the wife."

He cycled back to the café and ordered a cup of tea and a doughnut, sitting this time with his back to the factory. Perhaps the security guard was simply overzealous. Still, it was something to report.

Early that evening, Charles Fraith was fumbling for his keys to Agatha's cottage.

A heavy hand fell on his shoulder. "What are you doing?" demanded a Scottish voice. Charles swung round. A police sergeant was standing, glaring at him.

"I'm a friend of Mrs. Raisin," he said crossly. "I usually have the keys to her cottage, but I forgot that they had been stolen. What are you doing here?"

"I am Sergeant Tulloch, following orders. A policeman will be along soon to relieve me."

"What has she been up to?" asked Charles, ringing the doorbell.

Agatha answered it. "It's all right, Sergeant," she said. "Come in, Charles. Sergeant, would you like a cup of tea?"

"Thanks, missus. Grand. Still hot out here."

"You might have given me a new set of keys," complained Charles, following Agatha into the kitchen.

"I like the feeling of not having to find you in residence when I get home," said Agatha. "Wait till I make that copper a cup of tea and I'll tell you what's been happening."

She made a pot of tea and then arranged it with milk, sugar and a plate of biscuits and carried it outside. She then brought out a canvas chair and told him to make himself comfortable.

When she returned, Agatha explained about the interest in her cottage and Country Fashions. "So Bill decided to give me a police guard," she ended. "I'd love to get inside that factory."

"What about James? He was always a dab hand at breaking and entering."

"He's gone off somewhere and left his keys with Mrs. Bloxby. Didn't even have the decency to tell me where he was going."

"He's a travel writer. He has to travel, Aggie."

"Don't call me Aggie."

"Heard from Roy?"

Agatha sighed. "I did try to talk to him on the phone, but he screeched, 'This is dangerous. *They* could be listening,' and rang off."

"He went through a lot, and he is a bit of a rabbit. So you think it might be the vulgar Bulgars?"

"Patrick's experience alone makes them look fishy to me. Maybe I could go in disguise and get a job in their factory."

"You! A lot of their stuff is hand-stitched. I bought one of their jackets. Mind you, they do fleeces and things like that. Can you work a sewing machine? No, of course you can't. Forget it."

"I can't send Toni. Too dangerous."

"I saw Simon the other day," said Charles. "The wedding's tomorrow. Are you going?"

Agatha flushed miserably. "If only he'd get out of the army, then I wouldn't mind. I suppose I'd better go."

"Has he been in touch with Toni?"

"Oh, I hope all that is over. She doesn't

seem heartbroken."

"Is Patrick winkling any information out of the police?" asked Charles.

"They seem to have clammed up, although Patrick says that it's probably because they're not getting anywhere and really do have nothing to tell him. Wait a bit. I wonder if that sergeant outside has any little bits of information. I'll just see if he wants any more tea."

Soon Charles faintly heard Agatha's voice coming from outside, saying, "Hey, wake up! You're supposed to be on guard." And then a wail of "Charles!"

He ran out to join her. Tulloch was slumped in his chair, his eyes closed. Charles felt for a pulse and heaved a sigh of relief. "He's not dead. Someone must have put something in his tea. I'll get the police and ambulance."

"Hurry up!" Agatha looked around wildly. "If he's only drugged, that meant someone wanted access to the house. Let go inside and lock the door."

"We can't leave him here baking in the sun. Get me an umbrella and I'll hold it over him. You phone the police. Do something and don't stand there like a stuffed fish."

■ ■ ■ ■

One hour later, Mrs. Bloxby opened the door of the vicarage to a deputation from the Ladies Society. Mrs. Ada Benson had obviously elected herself as spokeswoman.

"We are here," she boomed, "to complain about the mayhem Agatha Raisin is causing in this village. Most of us ladies retired here for a quiet life."

"What has happened?" asked the vicar's wife.

"A policeman on guard outside her cottage has been found unconscious. She has brought *terror* to this village. She should be asked to leave."

"Poor Mrs. Raisin!" exclaimed Mrs. Bloxby. "I must go to her right away."

"And you'll tell her to leave?"

Mrs. Bloxby pushed past the women and said over her shoulder, "If it hadn't been for the superb detective activities of Mrs. Raisin in the past, then you really would find this a terrifying place. Don't be silly, Mrs. Benson."

"I'm resigning from the Ladies Society," shouted Mrs. Benson.

Mrs. Bloxby's voice floated back to her as she turned the corner. "Good!"

■ ■ ■ ■

Agatha's cottage was a hive of activity. Police cars blocked Lilac Lane, and white-suited men were carefully dusting Agatha's front door for fingerprints. A policeman volunteered the information that Mrs. Raisin and her friend had gone to the pub.

Mrs. Bloxby found Agatha and Charles in the pub garden. Agatha was smoking furiously, a carton of Bensons she had bought in the village store in front of her.

Charles explained what had happened. When he had finished, Agatha said, "I am the number one suspect. I took him the tea. Nobody saw a soul outside my cottage. Miss Simms, you know, the secretary of the Ladies Society, well, her latest gentleman friend had given her a present of a nasty little yappy dog. She walked it along Lilac Lane, called hullo to Tulloch, went to the end where it meets the fields, turned back and saw what she thought was Tulloch asleep. She didn't meet anyone either going or coming. So I'm sitting here, drinking gin and smoking myself to death with nerves. I'm supposed to be on my way to headquarters with Charles to make a complete statement. But I told them I needed a short break first, and do you know what the bastards did? They confiscated my passport. Every time they don't know what to do with me, they take away my passport and I usually have to hire a lawyer to get it back."

"They can't possibly think you had anything to do with it. Would you like me to come with you?"

"That's kind of you," said Agatha. "But they'll want to interview Charles as well, so we may as well suffer together."

Mrs. Bloxby walked thoughtfully back to the vicarage. She sat down at her computer and began to type out a poster. It said: "From the Vicarage. Ladies Society meetings will no longer be held in the vicarage. If you wish to continue, you will need to find somewhere else. I am resigning. Margaret Bloxby."

I am not going around on this hot day, shoving separate notes through letterboxes, she thought. I'll take this to the shop and put it up on the notice board.

She was just pinning it up when Miss Simms came to join her. "Well, if you ain't going to be around, I'm handing in my resignation as well," she said. Miss Simms was still damned with the title of Carsely's unmarried mother, which Mrs. Bloxby found grossly unfair considering that being unmarried seemed to be a growth industry. Young girls in Mircester got pregnant knowing the council would supply them with a flat and allowances. Often it was a way of escaping from brutal parents. Other times, it was prompted by laziness.

"It's not as if there are any ladies anymore, know what I mean?" said Miss Simms. "It's all pushy newcomers now like Mrs. Benson. They come and they go. House prices go up and they sell and a new lot comes in. They want the village dream, so they join the Ladies Society and we all sit around eating cakes an' bitching. Oh, jeez, I am sorry." For her little dog had peed into Mrs. Bloxby's shoes.

"It's said to be lucky," said Mrs. Bloxby. Mrs. Tutchell, the shop owner, produced a roll of kitchen paper, and Mrs. Bloxby dried her ankles and shoes. "Are you sure there was no one in or near Lilac Lane?"

"Swear to God. I felt like inventing someone just so as to help Mrs. Raisin, but that was afterwards. I didn't know she'd get into trouble."

"They cannot possibly think she would be so mad as to dope that sergeant's tea," said Mrs. Bloxby.

"Maybe someone sneaked in and put

something in the tea caddy."

"Mrs. Raisin uses teabags."

"Well, what about that security firm that changed the locks a' all that?"

"Vetted thoroughly by the police."

"Oh, well, she's tough. She'll stand up to the police. So it's goodbye to the Ladies Society?"

"As far as I am concerned. Such an old-fashioned name."

"Don't them over in Ancombe still call it a ladies society?"

"No. They've changed the name to the Forward Women's Group."

"I'd better get on and take this pet rat with me."

"I see it's a Chihuahua," said Mrs. Bloxby.

Miss Simms giggled. "Is it really? Funny, that. That's what one of my gentlemen friends called my . . ." Her voice trailed off before Mrs. Bloxby's clear gaze. "Oh, gotta go."

"Do you want me to stay the night?" asked Charles.

"Yes, thanks," said Agatha as they at last emerged from police headquarters into the fading sunlight.

"I'd better go home first and get my togs for tomorrow," said Charles.

"Tomorrow?"

"Simon's wedding."

"Snakes and bastards! I'd better find something to wear."

"Go to the office when you've found something," said Charles, "and wait for me. We'll go to your cottage together."

"Thanks." A tear rolled down Agatha's cheek.

"Come on, old girl, this isn't like you. Where's your stiff upper lip?"

"As *The Goon Show* once memorably said, it's over my loose wobbly lower one," said Agatha, taking out a crumpled tissue and dabbing her eyes. "I wonder what drug was given to Tulloch and how it got there?"

"Forensics, like the mills of God, grind slowly. We won't hear for a bit."

Once in her office, Agatha got a call from her cleaner, Doris Simpson, to say she had taken Agatha's cats home with her. "Men in white suits all over the place," said Doris. "And they could have been trodden on with those policemen and their big boots."

Agatha thanked her, wondering how on earth she had managed to forget the welfare of her cats.

Sitting down with a pile of files covering both murders, Agatha began to read through them, looking for any sort of clue. Fiona Richards had been in the George when Staikov was there. Was there a connection?

Phil had left a note saying he was watching the Richardses' house but had taken pains to make sure he would not be recognised.

If I could solve Beech's murder, then everything else might fall into place, thought Agatha. It was a particularly vicious murder. Revenge? Hate? A warning? And how could he possibly have been any use to them apart from turning a blind eye to speeding and parking violations?

Patrick went into a Richards Supermarket in Mircester and began to look around. It was an example of the sort of giant supermarket that was slowly killing off the small shops in Mircester, as it sold everything from food to pots and pans, clothes and takeaway meals. He remembered he needed a new shirt to wear to Simon's wedding and headed for the clothes section.

There was a placard in front of the section with the legend THE CHEAPEST YOU CAN BUY! LOOK AT OUR LEATHER JACKETS!

"I wonder," muttered Patrick. He lifted down one of the jackets and examined the label. It did not say "Country Casuals." Instead it simply had a small label saying "Richards." It was not good leather. The jackets were made of the type of leather that looked almost like plastic and was stiff and unyielding.

Could there be a connection with Staikov's firm?

CHAPTER TEN

Only Charles, in full morning dress, seemed to have made an effort for the occasion of Simon's wedding. Agatha had not found anything suitable to wear in Mircester and had not been allowed back into her cottage the evening before. In the morning she had rapidly scrambled into a pale blue trouser suit, realising only when she got to the church how much she hated it. Although it was well designed, she felt pale blue was definitely not her colour.

Roy, who had been invited, had sent his apologies, probably frightened he might be abducted again. Mrs. Freedman was resplendent in black-and-red-patterned silk and with a large straw hat decorated with silk poppies. Patrick and Phil were in lounge suits. Toni looked subdued. She was wearing a dark grey silk dress, rather drab, as if she were wearing half mourning, like an Edwardian lady. Mrs. Bloxby was there with her husband, wearing the same outfit she had worn to many weddings: an unflattering brown chiffon dress and a large straw hat decorated with brown chiffon roses.

As if by common consent, they all shuffled into pews at the very back of the church. Agatha, worried about Toni, hoped the service would not be too long. There was to be a reception afterwards at Simon's parents' home. They had all decided, for Toni's sake, to forgo it.

For her part, Toni really did not know what she felt.

Many of Simon's regimental friends were in the church, reminding guilty Agatha that it was surely her fault that he had gone to Afghanistan.

The church was very warm. Agatha began to regret she had jeered so many times about global warming. The stained-glass windows of the abbey sent down harlequin shafts of light. The organ played softly.

Charles whispered, "What's happening? Simon isn't here. The best man's there, but no Simon." People began to twist their heads, looking anxiously towards the door.

Agatha experienced a sudden feeling of dread. She whispered to Patrick, "What if he's been kidnapped like Roy?"

"Probably sleeping off the effects of some

stag party," replied Patrick comfortably.

Agatha craned her neck. She could see what must be Simon's father talking urgently to some of Simon's army colleagues. They left the abbey.

A babble of conversation rose up to the hammer beams on the roof. One woman left the church for a few minutes and then came back and announced excitedly, "Poor Susan is in the wedding car, being driven around and around. Where is the wretched boy?"

Agatha was just about to go outside and phone Bill when Simon's army colleagues came back into the church and went straight up to his father. There was a frantic discussion, and then Simon's father announced, "I am sorry. The wedding is off."

People rose from their pews and began to stream out through the great double doors of the abbey. But Agatha, followed by Charles, thrust her way through the departing guests and approached Simon's father.

"Has Simon been found?" she gasped.

"Yes, he has," he answered curtly. "He has been found at our home. I have much to do. Please excuse me."

Thank God he's at least safe, thought Agatha. She made her way back to Toni. "Have you still got Simon's mobile phone number?"

"Yes," said Toni.

"Please phone him and find out what the matter is."

"He probably won't answer," said Toni. "Oh, don't glare at me. I'll try."

Toni went out and stood in the shade of a tall tombstone and called. Simon answered. "It's Toni. Where are you?"

"I've locked myself in my room. I couldn't go through with it."

"Why?"

"My father doesn't believe in stag parties, and we had a small party last night for the family and relatives. I was teasing Sue about names for the baby and telling her she shouldn't drink so much. She said she'd had an abortion because otherwise she wouldn't have fitted into her wedding dress. Look, the reason I proposed was because she said she was pregnant."

"So why didn't you just put a stop to everything there and then?"

"I hadn't the courage. So many arrangements."

Toni could hear someone banging and shouting, "Come out of there immediately!"

"Got to go," he said, and rang off.

Toni returned to her colleagues and told

them what Simon had said. "Of all the wimps!" exclaimed Agatha.

"You got him into this," said Toni. "If it hadn't been for your interference, he'd never have joined the army."

"That's unfair," said Charles quietly. "Next thing you'll be telling us that Agatha got Sue pregnant."

"Sorry," Toni mumbled.

"Well, I'm going back home to get out of this hot clobber. Oh, look. Here comes James."

James, as impeccably dressed as Charles, came hurrying up. "Have I missed the wedding?"

They rapidly explained to him what had happened. "It was a bit of a dirty trick to tell him at the very last moment," said James roundly. "I would say he's well out of it. I'm hungry. Anyone want lunch?"

Aware of Agatha's beady eyes on them willing them to go away, they all muttered apologies. "I'm free," said Agatha cheerfully. "Let's go."

Over an Italian meal, Agatha told James what had been happening. "I feel it's all to do with that factory of Staikov's. I wish we could get in there. Patrick says it's well guarded. Now, that's suspicious."

"Not necessarily," remarked James. "Lots of expensive leather to guard."

"I'd love to get in there and have a look."

"Agatha! I'm through with breaking and entering. What we could do . . ."

"Yes?" How Agatha loved the sound of that "we."

"If there's any nefarious business going on, it would probably take place at night. We could go up there after midnight and have a look."

"Oh, James, thank you. When you just cleared off, I thought you'd lost interest."

"I have to make a living."

"But you have independent means."

"True, but I feel pretty useless when I'm not working, and I enjoy the travel. I'm about to do something new. Next month, I'm doing a feature film for the BBC on British expats who sold up here and moved to Spain to start a new life."

"You're going to be a television presenter! I could handle the publicity for you."

"No, Agatha. I prefer a quiet life."

Agatha studied him, her mind a whirl of thoughts. He would have researchers, camera crew, make-up girl, all the usual circus. Some of the girls might be very pretty. She pulled herself together and told herself not to be silly.

214

"I'm thinking of closing down the agency for two weeks and giving everyone a holiday," said Agatha. "I don't want to put any of them in danger."

"Good idea. Talking about danger, I hope Simon doesn't start chasing after Toni again."

"He behaved disgracefully."

"Not quite. He should have called off the whole thing the night before, the minute he knew she wasn't pregnant. Still, he's very young. And would it be so very bad if he and Toni got together?"

"I think he's unstable," said Agatha mulishly. "Let's make plans for tonight."

"Where's Charles?"

"Gone off home. You know Charles. He flits in and out of my life and I never know when I am going to see him next."

Toni heard her doorbell ring at nine that evening. Because Agatha was paying her a good wage, she had invested in an intercom.

"Who is it?" she asked.

"Simon."

Toni hesitated for a moment and then pressed the buzzer to let him in.

Then she opened the door and watched him mount the stairs. "I didn't think they'd let you out after the mess you created," she said.

"Don't you start. I've had enough of it." Simon crossed the room and slumped into an armchair. With his odd jester features, he looked like a discarded puppet.

Toni shut the door and then sat down in an armchair facing him. "You could have had children once you were married."

"Fact is," said Simon, running a weary hand through his thick hair, "I'd begun to go off her. We drink a lot in the regiment, but once we got back to Mircester, she just kept on drinking buckets. She's pretty coarse when she's drunk."

"So why wait until the last minute?"

"I just panicked. I want out of the army."

"Why did you join up in the first place?"

Toni dreaded hearing him say "It was because of you."

But he sighed and shifted uneasily in his chair. "I'd begun to find the detective work boring. I don't like working for women, and Agatha is not the most sympathetic of creatures."

"So it wasn't because of me?"

"I'd like to flatter you, but no, it wasn't. But now I'm free, we can start to see each other."

"I don't want to anymore," said Toni.

216

"And don't pretend to look miserable. Own up, Simon! You want a shoulder to cry on."

He grinned suddenly. "You always were sharp. Anyway, Dad's fixed up for me to see a shrink."

"Why? Because of Sue?"

"No, I want out of the army, and a sympathetic family shrink friend is going to diagnose me with post-traumatic stress."

"But won't the army want to examine you as well?"

"They won't get a chance. I'll be in a loony bin run by this psychiatrist. Mum doesn't want me to go back to Afghanistan."

"You're thoroughly spoilt," said Toni.

"I certainly am, and I plan to make the most of it."

"I think you'd better leave. I'm tired. I've got a lot to do tomorrow."

Simon stood up. He tried to kiss her, but she ducked her head and then went and held the door open.

When she had closed it behind him, she sat down and wondered if Agatha had been right about him all along.

Agatha and James drove off after midnight through the sleeping village of Carsely. "If this hot weather goes on," said James, "there'll be a hosepipe ban. How's your garden?"

"Fine," said Agatha defensively, thinking of her wilting plants that she kept forgetting to water.

"We'll need to park somewhere well outside the estate and walk," said James.

"It's pretty open ground all round," said Agatha.

"There is a bit of wood and scrub at the back. As far as I remember, not all the units are fenced off. I checked it out earlier after supper."

They drove on in silence. "Oh, look," said James as they neared the industrial estate. "There are clouds building up in the west."

"I hope there's not going to be another storm like there was on the night Roy was kidnapped," said Agatha, thinking all the while, What if James is a success as a television personality? He'll be famous. There will be beautiful women after him. Look at the way he nearly married that airhead. But does it matter anymore? She felt that old obsession she once had for him was being aroused by the competitive streak in her nature. But then she remembered all the hurt and jealousy and sheer misery that obsession had brought her, and she gave a dry little sob.

James stopped the car abruptly. "Are you

all right? Severed heads and murders are enough to shake the strongest person."

"I'm fine," said Agatha defiantly. "Press on."

James took a small earthy track leading round to the back of the industrial site. He switched off the headlights and parked just inside.

The site had once been a camp for Polish refugees during World War II. Old people remembered when the Poles had their own shops and even a cinema. Most of the businesses were now in old Nissen huts. But Country Fashions was a large, square brick building with a staff entrance at the side and a loading bay at the back.

"You see that mound of grass and earth over there?" whispered James. "We can lie behind it and get a good look at the loading bay."

"It's clouding over," Agatha whispered back.

"I brought a couple of night vision binoculars," said James, opening a travel bag. He handed a pair to Agatha. "Now, we wait."

The night dragged on. Clouds covered the moon, and then a light rain began to fall. "Let's give up," moaned Agatha.

"Keep your voice down. I can hear something coming. Here comes the security guard."

The rumble of a vehicle drew nearer. The guard opened the gates to the loading bay. A thickset man came out of the building. "Evening, Mr. Staikov," said the guard.

"That must be the son," whispered Agatha. "He's taken over the business."

The truck rumbled to a stop. The back doors were opened and two men jumped out. The driver and another man who had been in the front seat came to join them.

They began to unload rolls of leather from the back and carry them into the building. Then they heard Staikov say clearly, "Bring the paperwork into the office and I'll sign it. I want to get to my bed. You were expected this afternoon."

"Bloody French," said one man. "Strike at Calais. Held us up for hours, it did."

Agatha felt a sinking feeling of disappointment. The load should have arrived in broad daylight. Staikov was inside signing paperwork. The rain was coming down heavier.

She tried to get to her feet, but James pulled her down. "We can't risk being seen. Wait until they drive off."

To Agatha, it seemed to take ages. Her soaking hair was plastered to her head. Her clothes were drenched.

At long last, the truck drove off, the gates were closed, and James said they could move.

In the car, he turned on the heater. "This is awful," moaned Agatha.

"It's good for the gardens."

"I'm not a plant!"

Although she knew she was risking valuable business, Agatha told her assembled staff in the morning that she was closing down the agency for two weeks. She said they had been under threat for too long and it would do them all good to get a break.

There were a few grumbles that she hadn't really given them time to make holiday arrangements, yet each of them was secretly relieved. Ever since Agatha had been sent that severed head and Roy kidnapped, they had all felt uneasy.

"Where will you go?" Toni asked Agatha.

"Don't know. I think I'd like to potter around, have tea with Mrs. Bloxby, do village things."

"Doesn't sound like you," remarked Phil.

"Well, I'm weary of the whole business. Maybe if I just switch off from it all, something will occur to me."

"We have cases outstanding," Mrs. Freedman pointed out.

"Nothing that can't be put on hold. Nothing really but nasty divorces. If we had an outstanding one about a missing child, then that would be different."

Toni went to her computer and looked up a Web site that offered last-minute holidays. Last-minute or not, the prices seemed high. She went out to find a travel agent. The pavements were steaming under the hot sun after last night's rain. It's almost tropical, thought Toni. She walked to a small travel agency at the corner of the street, pushed open the door and went in.

"Hi, Tone," a voice greeted her.

Toni saw Chelsea Flitter, the girl she had last seen working as a receptionist at Mixden's detective agency. "What are you doing here?" asked Toni.

"It's better here. You get free trips. I'm off to Las Vegas."

"Oh, you lucky thing!" exclaimed Toni. "I've always wanted to play the tables, just once."

"Here, you could do it!" said Chelsea excitedly. "I'm off tonight. It's a holiday agency called Summerflight. They've got their own planes. Leaves Gatwick Airport. Only four days. You could share my room. All you'd need is the money for the ticket and I can book that now. It'll be more fun

222

with two of us. Come on, Tone. We may even meet a couple of millionaires."

"I'll do it," said Toni.

"Attagirl!"

The flight was uncomfortable at first, the computer having crammed the passengers into all the seats at the front. Anything to eat or drink had to be purchased, and they even had to put one pound in the slot to use the toilet. Fortunately, the plane was only half-full and they were able to find other seats and stretch out.

The hotel was called the Old Prairie Ranch and was on the outskirts of Las Vegas near the airport. The architecture could be described as Plastic Log Cabin. Their room opened out onto a dusty outside corridor. It had a tired look. A cockroach lurked in the shower. Toni began to wish she had not come, but nothing seemed to dim Chelsea's enthusiasm.

"You know, I've always admired you, Tone," she said. "If I went a bit easier on the war paint and brushed my hair down, we could look like sisters."

Toni was tired and suggested they should have a few hours' sleep before setting off into town.

They ordered hamburgers and Cokes

from room service, and then both fell into a heavy sleep.

Toni was awakened by Chelsea shaking her. "Show a leg, girl. Time to hit the town."

Las Vegas *was* exciting as their taxi deposited them at the Rio Grande Hotel and Casino. There was a hectic buzz in the air. The whole city seemed a symphony of flashing neon lights.

Toni was wearing a simple black sheath with a row of pearls around her neck. Chelsea had also put on a black dress and had toned down her make-up. At first, as they entered, Toni felt almost overdressed. Elderly men and women were crouched at the slot machines, their eyes glazed, pulling the levers.

"I want to play roulette," said Toni.

But Chelsea had noticed that the people at the machines were not all old. A young man with a cowboy hat pushed back on his head winked at her. "You go play roulette," said Chelsea. "I'll try my luck here."

"What if we lose each other?" protested Toni.

"I've got a mobile which can work here. What about you?"

"Yes, I've got one of those."

"Good, we can text each other."

Feeling very young and self-conscious,

Toni made her way to the roulette tables after buying a modest amount of chips. Not knowing whether she was allowed to use a camera or not, she still wanted a record of her visit. Agatha had given her a present of a "spy" camera in the shape of a cigarette lighter. Toni had it inside a clutch handbag. She fished it out along with a packet of cigarettes. No one seemed to be smoking. Was there a smoking ban? Never mind, she told herself, if someone thinks I'm going to light up, I'm sure they'll stop me. She rapidly clicked off a series of photographs of the people around the roulette tables. Then she saw a place at a table where she could push in.

She put fifty dollars on thirteen, and to her amazement, she won. She then played another fifty on seven and won again. "Third time lucky, honey," said an excited woman beside her. Toni played on, she lost some, but then won again, and again. Common sense took over and she decided to stop playing.

"Luck hardly ever goes on happening," remarked Toni, gathering up her chips. When she cashed in her chips, she found she had won nearly two thousand dollars. She went off to find Chelsea, who was still feverishly playing the slot machines. "I've won quite a bit," said Toni. "Let's get something to eat."

"Later," muttered Chelsea. "I'll let you know."

Toni found a café serving snacks and settled down to eat. She noticed a few people were smoking. The café had a balcony overlooking the main floor of the casino. She shot some more pictures and then focussed on the slot machines where she had left Chelsea. She put away her camera and phoned her. The ringing stopped and went into voice mail. She texted her, saying she would meet her at the entrance. First, she searched along the rows and rows of slot machines without finding Chelsea.

Toni waited nervously at the entrance, standing next to a security guard for safety, saying she was waiting for her friend.

She became anxious. If Chelsea had met some man, surely she would have phoned or texted. Maybe her phone didn't work in the States after all.

At last, the sympathetic security guard got someone to take her up to the surveillance room. There were banks and banks of cameras photographing every part of the casino. Toni tried to estimate how long had passed since she had left Chelsea. Perhaps just over an hour. She pleaded to look at film of the slot machines around that time.

The film ran. Then she cried, "Stop! That's her!" Chelsea could be seen avidly pulling the handle of a slot machine. They ran the film forward. Chelsea rose. She was talking to someone, looking surprised and then anxious. She said something and took out her phone. Then she shook her head. Her companion said something else. Chelsea looked startled. With her new companion, she moved towards the entrance. Chelsea kept looking wildly round as if seeking help. They disappeared outside the casino.

"Are there cameras outside?" asked Toni. The operator switched over to the outside. Chelsea was thrust into the driver's seat of a Lexus and then scrambled over to the passenger side. The car drove off.

"Looks bad," said the operator heavily. "Stay where you are, little lady, and we'll get the cops."

"Can't you get a clear picture of that man?" cried Toni.

"He's got a baseball cap pulled right down. Could be anyone."

At first, the police tried to tell Toni that her friend had probably gone off with some man for a quickie and would soon be back.

"She's not like that," howled Toni. "Well, maybe. But she would have found me and told me. I'm telling you, she was frightened."

"We've got the number of the car," said a sergeant wearily. "Go back to your hotel and wait for her."

So Toni did just that. Once in her room, she phoned Agatha. "Who is this Chelsea?" demanded Agatha.

"Just someone I was at school with," said Toni. "It was a last-minute decision to go with her."

"What does she look like?"

"Well, blond, slim — in fact, she did herself up to look a bit like me. Said we'd look like sisters."

"Give me the number of your hotel. I'll go straight to police headquarters. I want still shots of that man from the casino. And the minute I've got that over with, I'm coming out to join you. What's your hotel like?"

"Horrible. It's called the Old Prairie Ranch."

"Sit tight in case she turns up."

Toni changed into a T-shirt and jeans, stretched out on the lumpy bed and waited. She thought the police would contact her again, but it seemed the case of a young girl going off with a man was hardly top priority.

She fell into an uneasy sleep and woke late in the morning. She asked the clerk in reception to contact the Las Vegas Police Department for her and waited anxiously. She was passed from one voice to another. When she finally got someone who knew about Chelsea's disappearance, he tried to reassure her that her friend had probably gone off on a one-night stand and would soon turn up. She was urged to give it more time. When the sergeant was interrupted, she was just being told not to be impatient. He barked, "Hold the line." When he came back on again, he said, "Two of our detectives are coming out to talk with you, miss."

Movement at last, thought Toni. She went downstairs to the reception area. Traffic going into Las Vegas roared past on the road outside, which shimmered in the heat. Then a black car drove up and two men got out. "Miss Gilmour?" they demanded as Toni rushed out to meet them.

"May I see your identification?" demanded Toni.

She studied their badges and said, "Let's go inside."

One detective was as thin as the other was fat. The thin one introduced himself as

229

Wight Bergen and the other as Parry Hyer. They explained they had received a call from England, and there was a suspicion that Chelsea had been abducted in mistake for Toni. Search and Rescue were out over the desert, looking for any sign of her.

They were efficient and courteous. Toni found it something of a relief to tell the two attentive detectives the story of the murders and the abduction of Roy from the beginning.

She had just finished when a taxi screeched to a halt outside the hotel. "Snakes and bastards!" came a familiar voice. "Was that as fast as this clapped-up wreck could go?"

"Look, lady, pay up and shut up."

"My boss," said Toni, running out to meet Agatha. Never before had she been so glad to see Agatha's abrasive presence.

Agatha paid the driver, adding, "And no tip to you for being so damned cheeky, and I bet you went the long way round."

"There are two detectives here," said Toni as the driver gave Agatha the finger and roared off. "You were quick."

"Got the first plane out, and you're hours behind England here."

Toni took Agatha's bag from her. Agatha's bearlike eyes surveyed the hotel. "I'll see these detectives and then we'll get out of this fleapit."

"But if Chelsea comes back, she'll expect to find me here!"

"We'll leave her a note. We'll book into that hotel where the casino is."

Agatha was introduced to the detectives.

"Your assistant has already explained everything to us," said Parry.

"Is there any chance of getting some stills from the video of Chelsea being taken from the casino?" asked Agatha.

"We already have some. We'll take you along to headquarters and you can have a look. Think you might recognise someone?"

"It's a slim hope," said Agatha. "Run and pack your bag, Toni. Do you need to settle your bill?"

"I've just a bit of room service to pay for. The rest was part of a package deal."

"I'll see to that. Get your case."

Soon they were on their way to the Las Vegas Police Department on Sunrise Avenue. Agatha and Toni studied the still photographs. The man seemed to know where the cameras were because he kept his head bent down and the long peak of his baseball cap pulled over his eyes. Despite the fact that the images were very good, they could make out only the line of his mouth and the fact that he was wearing a light jacket over chinos and baseball boots.

"May I keep one of these?" asked Agatha.

"Sure," said Parry. "We've e-mailed plenty to . . . where's the damn place, Murchester?"

"Mircester."

"Whatever. We found the Lexus abandoned. It had been stolen. We'll phone you as soon as we hear anything. You'll be staying at the Rio Grande?"

"Yes," said Agatha.

"Have a good one."

"As if we could," muttered Agatha in the back of the police car that was taking them to their hotel.

"Agatha," said Toni suddenly, "I didn't tell them, I took photographs while I was in the casino. I didn't know whether it was legal or not."

"Is it that spy camera I gave you?"

"Yes."

"Let's keep that to ourselves. We'll get your photos when we get home."

They checked into a double room, ordered food from room service and waited, and waited.

Agatha, suffering from jet lag, fell asleep

and jerked awake an hour later when the phone rang.

Toni answered it. Agatha heard her say, "What? . . . Where? . . . Is she all right? . . . We'll be there directly."

When she put the phone down, Toni's face was glowing with relief. "A helicopter found her staggering around Death Valley and picked her up. She's in the Lutheran hospital. Let's go."

Chelsea turned out to be suffering from heat exhaustion and sunburn. Agatha and Toni had to wait until the police had finished interrogating her. Then it was their turn.

Chelsea turned furious eyes on Toni out of her sun-scorched face. "It's all your fault," she howled.

"How on earth . . . ?" began Toni.

"He thought I was you, see? He drove out with a gun in my side, and then he said, 'You had it coming to you, Toni Gilmour.' I screamed I wasn't you and that my passport was in me bag. He stopped the car, told me to hand over my bag, fished out me passport and began to curse something awful. Then he says, 'Get out, bitch.' I got out and ran and ran away from the road as fast as I could. I wandered around and around. I could see lights from cars away on the road, but I was frightened to go back in case he got me again. Then the helicopter picked me up. Let me tell you something, Tone. I never want to see you again. You can chase the bad guys as much as you want, but keep me out of it. You could have warned me."

"How could she have warned you?" said Agatha. "She didn't know there was any danger here. How could she?"

"Bet she did. Piss off, both of you." Chelsea turned her face away.

After that visit, Chelsea refused to see them again. Her handbag had been found and her passport was still there, lying on the ground beside it. Parry told Agatha and Toni that Chelsea was leaving in two days' time.

"Did she say anything useful about the man?" asked Agatha. "What sort of accent?"

"She just said he had a growly voice and she thought he was foreign. She said he smelled of booze. That's all she knows." He turned to Toni. "Miss Gilmour, are you sure your decision to come here was made at the last minute?"

"Sure as sure. Agatha decided to close the agency for two weeks because we were all afraid someone might be out to get us. I met Chelsea just by chance and she persuaded me to come on the trip. I think I want to go home now."

"Me too," said Agatha. "Let whining little Chelsea make her own way."

"You are pretty harsh, ma'am. She's a very young girl who's had a bad fright."

"Well, I can do bugger all for her when she won't even see me or let me help," howled Agatha.

Parry looked at her with dislike. Ball-breaking old trout, he thought. Aloud, he said, "Let us know which flight you will be on."

"We should really be around to take care of her," protested Toni.

"It's you they're after, not her," said Agatha. "Oh, well, one last try. Back to the hospital."

"I'll go," said Toni quickly. "She might speak to me if you're not there."

"Ask her how he got her to leave with him."

"He had a gun."

"He couldn't have taken a gun into the casino. He must have said something else."

Toni had noticed a medical supply shop near the hospital. She bought a white lab coat and a stethoscope. In an adjacent tourist shop, she bought a square badge with the legend I LOVE LAS VEGAS.

In the hospital, she went to the toilets and locked herself in a cubicle, where she put on the white coat and hung the stethoscope around her neck. She then took out a pair of nail scissors from her pocket and prised open the badge. Fortunately, it was blank on the other side. She printed "Dr. Finlay" neatly in black ink. It would have to do. She had left her handbag at the hotel, carrying money and the scissors in her trouser pocket so that she would not have to find a place to hide a handbag.

Toni walked through the hospital corridors. She walked quickly past the policeman on guard outside Chelsea's door, giving him an efficient nod.

Chelsea opened her mouth to scream, but Toni said hurriedly, "You scream and I'll tell your mum about that fling you had with the sales rep from Birmingham."

"You wouldn't!"

"Try me."

"Wadda ya want?" demanded Chelsea, who was trying very hard to obtain an American accent.

"Something more about the man who abducted you. He couldn't have got a gun into the casino or a knife. Why did you go off with him?"

"He said he was a detective and wanted a word with me outside."

"Did he have a badge?"

"No. One of them warrant cards."

"Did you get a close look at the card?"

"No, I just followed the guy out, like. Once in the car, he took out a gun, drove with one hand and pointed the gun at me with the other.

"He said, 'I'm going to shut your mouth for once and all, Toni Gilmour. How the hell did you know I was in Las Vegas? Who told you?'

"I began to cry and said it was a package deal. I wasn't Toni Gilmour, and he could look at my passport in my handbag if he didn't believe me. He stopped suddenly when we was out in the desert and he asks me to hand over my bag. He opens it, looks at me passport, swears something awful, chucks the bag out of the winder and tells me to get out. I ran for my life. Right into the desert. I'm going home tomorrow. The British consul has arranged it. So bugger off, Tone, and don't come near me again."

"One more thing. Did you tell the police about the warrant card?"

"Didn't remember until later."

"American police have badges. Only British police have warrant cards. Didn't you

237

think of that?"

"Piss off," howled Chelsea.

Agatha's eyes gleamed with excitement when Toni told her Chelsea's story. "Pack up," she said. "We're leaving today."

"But what about Chelsea?"

"Whoever it was wanted you, not her. She'll be safe."

Agatha and Toni had hoped to collect their cars from the airport terminal at Gatwick and get back to Mircester, but they were intercepted and taken to a room in the airport where two plainclothes detectives grilled them. Evidently, the Las Vegas police were angry that they had just disappeared while an investigation was in progress. They were taken through their stories again.

At last, they were released but warned that the Mircester police would be calling on them later.

"At least they didn't take my passport away again," grumbled Agatha. "Do you want to follow me to Carsely?"

"No, I'll go to my flat. I'm tired."

CHAPTER ELEVEN

Simon found that the army were only too glad to get rid of him. Sergeant Sue Crispin was popular, and they felt that Simon had behaved disgracefully.

He had made several attempts to see Toni again, but she always said she was too busy.

He even asked Agatha for his old job back, but Agatha said roundly she could not afford to take on any more staff.

Simon had always disliked authority figures, something that had landed him in trouble many times in his short army career. To him, Agatha Raisin was the epitome of an authority figure. He decided to apply to Mixden, Agatha's rival agency, for a job.

Mr. Mixden laid down the same terms he had laid down to Toni.

Simon hesitated only a minute. "All right," he said. "But I will expect a bonus if I get something really good."

"Then let's see how good you are," said

Mixden. "You're on a month's trial. Remember, no one's paying us to solve these murders. But I want the publicity."

Simon decided the best way to go about finding out what was happening over at Agatha's agency would be to pretend to be unemployed and get as friendly with Toni as possible.

At that moment, Toni and Agatha were studying the photographs taken from Toni's little camera, along with the still photos given to them by the Las Vegas police. They put them up on the computer screen in the office.

Patrick and Phil peered over their shoulders. "He's clever," said Patrick. "Look at the way he ducks his head. He knows exactly where the cameras are."

Agatha leaned back in her chair. "I wonder," she said slowly, "if it was all just some sort of coincidence. Say it's someone from around here, addicted to gambling. He spots what looks like Toni and thinks he's been found out. I mean, just look at Chelsea. She really did go out of her way to look like you, Toni. Say this chap sees Toni enter the casino. Then she's lost from view. *Then* he thinks he sees Toni playing the machines."

240

"If that's maybe the case," said Patrick, "it could be someone who likes money the way Beech did. And if he's got the gambling habit, he might be prepared to do anything for it."

Toni's mobile rang. It was Simon. "You seem to have been having a lot of adventures," he said. "What about meeting up this evening?"

"I'm a bit busy."

"Look, Toni, I'd really appreciate it. Everyone's treating me like a leper."

"Just a drink, then," said Toni. "Eight o'clock in the Dragon."

Charles Fraith had called at Agatha's cottage, thinking she would be resting up after her ordeal in Las Vegas. James Lacey had gone off on his travels again but had left Charles a copy of the notes from Gary Beech's ledger. Charles decided to walk along to the Red Lion, have a drink and see if he could make any sense of them.

He ordered a half of lager and sat at a table by the window. He gazed at the notes, but they didn't mean anything to him.

"Thousands of pounds, all gone. I'm going to have trouble with the insurance," said a voice.

Charles looked over. He recognised a

farmer called Ettrick who had recently bought a farm outside the village. The man he was speaking to said, "You mean they pinched a whole combine harvester?"

"The whole damn thing," complained Ettrick. "I phoned the insurance, but they're humming and hawing and said I shouldn't have left it out in the field with all the thefts of farm machinery that have been going on."

Charles glanced down at the notes. Could c.h. mean combine harvester? Could Beech have been alerting some gang as to where to go and what to steal?

"What would anyone want stealing a combine harvester?" asked Ettrick's companion.

"They do say they come in the night, dismantle the thing, load it up and it ends up somewhere in Eastern Europe. The Carters over at Broadway had their 'un pinched last year. That Beech, him who was murdered, he says it was their own fault. Ought to have locked it up for the night."

Charles finished his drink, went outside and phoned Agatha. When he had finished, her voice was sharp with excitement. "Beech must have been spying for some gang, telling them about houses that were easy to break into, telling them about where to pick up expensive farm machinery.

"Which means," Agatha concluded slowly, "that there might be another rogue cop. The man who abducted Chelsea showed a warrant card. I'd better get on to Bill."

To Agatha's disappointment, both Bill and Wilkes thought the whole thing was too farfetched, but at Agatha's insistence they promised to look into it. But when she had gone, Bill said, "It wouldn't do any harm to take a look at the coppers and see if any of them look more flush with money than the others. An awful lot of farm machinery has gone, along with expensive cars. We've had all the force out on these murders. Maybe it's time to get the files out on the theft and take another look."

The sad fact is that there is a division between town and country. Even in towns like Mircester, surrounded as it was by countryside, it was assumed all farmers were rich despite all the plagues that visited them, from mad cow disease to tuberculosis, and therefore the sometimes overworked police force of Mircester didn't put enough energy into solving cases like missing tractors and combine harvesters. Bill, drafting in help to go through back cases, was often met with the surly remark of "They're insured anyway," generally from those who did not realise the insurance was apt to go sky-high and that the recent government's heavy tax on four-by-fours had been an added burden. Wilkes obtained a search warrant for Country Fashions, and Customs & Excise were warned to search all of Staikov's trucks leaving or entering the country. He also ordered a search of the passenger lists on all aircraft going to or returning from Las Vegas.

Toni was relieved when she met Simon that evening to find him cheerful and friendly. "Got a job yet?" she asked.

"Looking around," said Simon airily. "How's the case going?"

"Which one?" asked Toni cautiously.

"You know, the murders and that pal of yours being kidnapped in Las Vegas."

"One minute Agatha tells us all to go on holiday in case something happens to one of us, and the next minute, we're all back on the job again."

"You can see her point. Until everything is solved, you'll always be looking over your shoulders. What's the latest?"

He looked so eager and friendly that Toni began to relax. There could be no harm in telling Simon. She often felt quite lonely in the evenings these days. Her old school friends seemed like strangers. She felt she had moved on out of their world: a world of discos and binge drinking and dreaming of becoming celebrities without getting any skills such as acting, singing or dancing.

So Toni told him all about the latest theory that the Las Vegas business might have been a coincidence, about the disappearing farm machinery, and about Agatha leaping to the conclusion that there might be another rogue cop who had taken over when Gary had been murdered.

Simon suggested they have dinner together, but Toni suddenly felt uneasy: that she should not have said anything at all. She swore him to secrecy, said she had another appointment and left.

After she had gone, Simon sat, thinking hard. Any policeman who had turned criminal would be careful not to flash money around. But if this bent copper — say he was a bent copper — had money, surely he would want to buy something special and maybe keep it hidden. The police would be checking the casinos of Britain, looking to see if there was a recognisable face, but that would take days and weeks of studying video footage.

He ordered another drink. Perhaps the best idea, he decided, would be to watch the comings and goings at police headquarters, see if there was something about any policeman that sparked his suspicions.

The police frequented a pub called the Golden Eagle round the corner from headquarters. He decided that it might be a better idea to go there.

But all he got for an evening's work was too much alcohol and a hangover the next morning. Not one policeman or detective seemed to be flush with money.

He drank two Alka-Seltzers and followed that with a cup of strong coffee before sitting down at his computer to type out a report for Mixden. Of course, he was cheating Agatha by spying for Mixden, but he comforted himself with the thought that Agatha deserved it for having interfered in his life.

As he was typing, his thoughts returned to what he, for example, would buy if he had a lot of money. A car, he suddenly thought. A Porsche, a Ferrari, something flash, keep it hidden but take it out for a spin on days off, keep it well away from Mircester in a lockup.

There was a dealer in expensive cars in Birmingham called Class Cars. He thought of phoning them but decided to go there in person. Thanks to the generosity of his parents, he had a wardrobe of expensive clothes. He put on a Savile Row suit with a silk shirt and silk tie, asked his father if he could borrow the Audi for a day and set off.

Once at Class Cars, he wandered around the showroom until an assistant came up and asked, "Can I help you, sir?"

Simon pretended to show interest in an Alfa Romeo. "I'm thinking of buying something really good," he said. "In this recession, you must be feeling the pinch."

"Well, I must admit, people are hanging on to the cars they've got," he said. "Would you like to take the Alfa out for a trial spin?"

"Look," said Simon, exuding sincerity, "I'll tell you what I'm really after." He produced one of the Agatha Raisin Detective Agency cards with his name on it. "I don't want to waste your time. You've read about those dreadful murders in the Cotswolds?"

"Yes, but what's that got to do with us?"

"It's a long shot," said Simon. "We feel we might be dealing with a bent copper. Now, he might just have spent some of his ill-gotten gains on a flash car. Can you remember anyone like that?"

The assistant hesitated and looked

around. The showroom was quiet. A secretary was working away in one corner. Another assistant was sitting staring moodily at a computer. Simon produced a roll of a hundred pounds.

"Put that away!" hissed the assistant. "It's just about my lunch hour. Let's go to a pub."

In the pub, it transpired his name was Wilfred Butterfield. Simon bought them drinks and found a quiet table in a corner.

"I'll take the money now," said Wilfred.

"I'll see if the info is worth it," said Simon.

"Well, we did have one chap. We joked afterwards that maybe he was a copper checking up on us. He had that look. Hard eyes, shiny black shoes, you know. He took one car after another out for a spin and then said, 'Maybe I'll be back.' Wasted a whole morning."

"What did he look like?"

"Thickset. Scottish accent. Fair hair."

Simon passed over the money. "Anyone else?"

"Nobody like that. Oh, we've sold cars, but all to reputable people."

"I wish I could have a look at your sales book."

"No. Absolutely not. That's going too far. Aren't you going to buy me lunch?"

"No," said Simon. "I've given you enough to buy your own."

On his way back to Mircester, Simon suddenly remembered there were several group photographs of police decorating the dingy Mircester police reception area. He headed straight for police headquarters and asked to speak to Bill Wong. He was told he was out.

"I might wait a bit and see if he comes back," said Simon. He strolled round, studying the photographs. Near the centre of one group was a burly man with sergeant's stripes and fair hair.

"Why!" he exclaimed. "I know this chap. Isn't that Henry James?"

The policeman on duty at the desk leaned over and peered at the photo. "Naw, that's our sergeant Billy Tulloch."

"Odd, that," said Simon. "Looks just like Henry James. I won't wait for Bill after all."

Simon waited in the car park outside all day, feeling hungrier and hungrier, but determined to get a look at Sergeant Tulloch. Then he saw him at nine o'clock in the evening. The sergeant got onto a powerful motorbike and set off. Simon followed in pursuit. At times he thought he had lost him because the sergeant cut down several winding side streets, but at last Simon saw him park outside a fairground on the outside of the town. Tulloch entered the fairground, and Simon followed him.

And then all at once he lost him among the fairground rides and booths.

He was standing, irresolute, when he felt something hard pressed into his side and heard a Scottish voice say, "This is a gun. Do as I say and nothing will happen to you."

He urged Simon towards a ride called the Haunted House. "Get in," muttered Tulloch. "Pay the fare."

Simon did as he was told. "Help me!" he mouthed at the man taking the money.

The man burst out laughing, thinking Simon was joking. The car jerked forward into the gloom. Halfway through the ride, a fake skeleton placed on a chair lurched forward. Tulloch drove a knife into Simon's side. The car stopped a moment before jerking forward. There was no one in the cars behind. Tulloch tore the skeleton from its chair and hauled Simon out onto the thin ramp used by the fairground engineers. He shoved Simon into the chair and then walked along the ramp to where there was a break in the canvas tent that covered the exhibit. He let himself out into the fairground and disappeared in the crowds.

Patsy Broadband and her boyfriend, Terry Kelly, climbed, giggling, into a car at the Haunted House. "We seem to be the only people here," said Patsy.

"Good," said Terry. "We can have a bit o' fun."

"Oh, go on! You are a one, ain't you? Just you be keeping your hands to yourself."

Halfway through the journey, Terry complained, "This is the least scariest place I've ever been in. Nothing but screeches and bits o' painted plastic."

The chair lurched to a halt. The chair holding Simon tipped forward and his body landed on top of them. Patsy screamed and screamed, "Get him offa me!"

"Better not. Get him out o' here," said Terry. "He's fainted or something."

The car lurched out into the garish light of the fairground.

"Hey. What's all this, then?" demanded the attendant.

"He fell out on us," said Terry.

"Oh, God, he's bleeding all over my new dress!" screamed Patsy, and went into strong hysterics.

An ambulance was called, the police were

called, and Simon, fluttering between life and death, was rushed to hospital.

CHAPTER TWELVE

Toni was just about to leave her flat when she was confronted by Alice Peterson. "You're to come with me to headquarters," she said. "Get in the car."

"What's up?" asked Toni.

"You'll find out when we get there," was all Alice would say.

"I thought it was only on TV that detectives refused to answer questions. Is Agatha all right and everyone at the agency?"

"Yes."

"And James and Charles?"

"Yes."

Toni worried and worried until she was at last in an interviewing room faced by Wilkes, Bill Wong and a policeman standing guard by the door.

Wilkes started the tape and then began. "Simon Black is in hospital in intensive care."

"What happened?"

253

"He was employed by Mixden's detective agency. We got a warrant to search his flat, and there on his computer was a full report of everything you had told him about Mrs. Raisin's suspicions that the murderer might be some policeman. The report was ready to be sent to Mixden."

"I once applied for a job there," said Toni, "but Mixden wanted me to spy on Agatha's agency for him. Oh, what on earth has Simon been up to? Will he live? Was he shot?"

"No, he was stabbed at the fairground and left to die inside the Haunted House. If he hadn't fallen forward across a couple, he would be dead by now. He lost a lot of blood. But the stab wound appears to have missed anything vital. We are waiting for him to come round."

"He told me he was unemployed!" said Toni, tears standing out in her eyes. "I've been such a fool."

"In your discussions, did he name anyone he suspected?"

"No. I would have told Agatha."

The questioning went on. Bill was sorry for Toni. Wilkes all but accused her of having an affair with Simon. Bill often wondered how pretty Toni could manage to maintain her air of innocence, considering the work she did and the things she had seen. He wondered if she were still a virgin. Maybe there were some left in this wicked day and age.

Toni was finally read out a statement and asked to sign it.

When she had left, Bill said, "You were a bit hard on her, sir."

"I am sick and tired of Agatha Raisin and her employees interfering with police work," said Wilkes.

"But it looks as if Mrs. Raisin's seemingly mad leap of intuition is going to be proved right."

"Who's been on holiday at the time Chelsea was taken in Las Vegas?"

"Just . . . Oh, what is it?"

The policeman at the door who had been talking to someone outside said urgently, "I think you'd better hear this, sir. There's a chap out in reception."

"Better be good," snarled Wilkes. Both he and Bill were suffering from lack of sleep.

Wilfred Butterfield rose to meet them as they walked into the reception area. He burst out with "As soon as I saw his photo on the telly, I knew it was my duty to come forward."

"Do you mean Simon Black?"

"Yes, he called at our showroom in

Birmingham. He said he worked for the Agatha Raisin Detective Agency. He showed me his card."

"And you are . . . ?"

"Wilfred Butterfield. Car salesman at Class Cars."

"You'd better come with us and make a statement."

In the interview room so recently vacated by Toni, Wilfred poured out his story, omitting any mention of the money Simon had given him.

When he had finished, Wilkes said, "Now let's get this straight. The man you described to Simon was thickset and had a Scottish accent."

"Yes."

There's only one here answers to that description, thought Wilkes, and that's Sergeant Tulloch. "Oh, now what is it?"

He left the room and came back, his face grimmer than ever. "Detective Sergeant Wong will get you to sign a statement. Thank you for coming forward. Please keep this information from the press."

Followed by Wilfred's fervent assurances, he left the room.

He was met by the desk policeman who had been on duty the night before. He listened to the tale of how Simon had asked for Bill Wong. Had been told he was out and had then said he would wait. Simon had studied the police photographs and then had pointed to one and asked if that was Henry James. The policeman had said it was Sergeant Tulloch and Simon had decided not to wait.

A search started for Tulloch. They were told it was his day off. Armed with a warrant, Bill, Wilkes, Alice and a squad of policemen descended on Tulloch's flat. There was no answer. Wilkes nodded and stood aside while the door was rammed open.

The small flat was empty. Wilkes put a call out for all airports and train stations to be watched along with the license plate of Tulloch's bike. He then waited out in the car while a team from Scenes of Crimes Operatives arrived to search the flat.

Toni went straight to the hospital as soon as she left police headquarters. She found Agatha in the waiting room. A little ways away from her sat Simon's parents.

"I'm sorry, Agatha," she whispered.

Agatha shrugged. "I've already endured a session with the police at dawn. So Simon was prepared to spy on us for Mixden's?

Well. Whatever he found out nearly killed him. What a waste of a bright young man. Don't blame yourself, Toni. That one could have fooled me as well. Oh, here comes the surgeon."

They watched anxiously and then saw smiles of relief on Simon's parents' faces. Wilkes and another detective they did not recognise arrived.

"You pair," said Wilkes. "There's no use waiting. Police and family only."

"I know. Let's phone Patrick," said Agatha. "I bet he's learned something."

They went to a café across the road where there were tables outside. Agatha ordered coffees for both of them, lit a cigarette and phoned Patrick.

Toni waited impatiently until Agatha had rung off. "The culprit appears to be a Sergeant Billy Tulloch. Either he was working with Beech or he took over when Beech left off. But he was working for someone or some gang. I hate being outside it all. There's nothing we can do but wait. For some reason, Simon visited a car salesroom in Birmingham and found out that someone of Tulloch's description had been asking about posh cars. Patrick says Staikov's place has been thoroughly checked and all his trucks as well. There's nothing more we can do today, and I need some sleep. I think you should stay with me tonight, Toni. My place is well guarded."

Toni hesitated only a moment. She thought of poor Simon, left to die in that horrible way. "Yes, thanks. I'll go home and pack a bag."

Toni was relieved to find Charles waiting outside Agatha's cottage in his car. She found undiluted Agatha rather overwhelming.

Over coffees, Charles listened to all the latest news. "I wonder what took Simon to that car showroom," said Charles. "Do you think Mixden knows more than he ought?"

"I think it was a leap of intuition," said Toni. "He probably tried to figure out what a copper with a lot of money that he couldn't splash about would think of doing with it."

"Patrick says that Tulloch wasn't due any holiday, just a few days off. That's probably why he went to Las Vegas."

"We've been concentrating on Staikov because his father is Bulgarian," said Agatha. "But what other firm has trucks going abroad?"

"Richards!" said Toni.

"He's stocking cheap leather jackets. He didn't need to get them from Staikov. I'm sure his trucks go abroad for fruit and veg as well. There are always protests in the local papers about supermarkets stocking foreign produce and ignoring the home-grown stuff."

There was a ring at the doorbell. "I'll go," said Charles. He looked through the spy hole. "It's Wilkes."

"Let him in," groaned Agatha. "What's happened now?"

But Wilkes had come to deliver a lecture. He believed in solid police procedure and felt Agatha's and Simon's wild flights of intuition were somehow cluttering up the investigation. In vain did Agatha point out that if it hadn't been for Simon, they would never have found out about Tulloch. She was told firmly that from now on, she and her staff were to leave matters strictly to the police.

When he had gone, Toni said, "We should have told him about our suspicions of Richards."

"I tell you what," said Agatha angrily, "I'm tired of that pompous twat treating me like a schoolgirl. I'll show him."

"How?" asked Charles.

"We'll all go to bed and have a good rest, and then we'll follow one of Richards' trucks and see where it goes."

"I'll see if James is at home," said Charles. "He's more of the derring-do type than I am."

But Charles returned shortly to say that James was not at home. "Oh, well," he said reluctantly, "I'd better go with you. If I were you, Agatha, I'd phone up Doris and ask her to come and collect your cats."

"Why?"

"I think what you are proposing is dangerous. Anyone who could employ a vicious psycho like Tulloch might make sure you don't stay alive."

They decided to tail one of the trucks during daylight, when there would be plenty of traffic on the road.

Agatha had recently bought a Mercedes, and they elected to use that, as Charles had a penchant for buying the cheapest second-hand car he could find.

They waited outside Richards Supermarket until they saw one of his large trucks move out. Charles was driving the Mercedes.

"If it's going to call in at local farms to pick up milk and stuff, we'll have wasted a day," he said.

But the truck rolled steadily southward. "He's taking the Dover road," said Agatha excitedly. "If they take the ferry, we'd better stay in the car."

But before Dover, the truck swung off the main road. "The traffic's thinner here," said Charles. "I'd better hang back a bit. We're right in the open countryside. Look, they're pulling into that lay-by. I'd better go on past, park somewhere and walk back and try to spy out what they're doing."

He drove on and parked up a farm track under a stand of trees. "There was a hedge opposite that lay-by," he said. "If we cross over into that field opposite and make our way back, we should be able to see what's going on."

Soon they were huddled behind the hedge. Several very tough-looking men had descended from the truck and were sitting beside the road, drinking coffee out of flasks and eating sandwiches. Agatha's stomach gave such a loud rumble, she was frightened they would hear it.

The day dragged on. The driver then got into the cab, but instead of starting up the engine, he settled himself down to sleep. The others climbed into the back of the truck, and then all was silence.

"There must be something up," whispered Toni. "I mean, what are they waiting for?"

The sun finally descended slowly down the sky. Charles was asleep, and Toni felt her eyes drooping. Only Agatha, smarting over Wilkes's lecture, kept her eyes fastened avidly on the truck.

At last she nudged Charles awake. "I can hear a car coming," she whispered. "Keep down!"

Headlights cut through the night. A car came to a halt. A man got out and banged on the doors of the truck.

"Who is it?" asked Toni.

The man moved into the headlights of his car. "It's Richards," said Agatha excitedly.

Tom Richards spoke to the driver. The truck moved off slowly. Richards got into his car and followed.

"Let them get away and we'll try to catch up with them," said Charles. "I'll need to drive without the headlights on in case they see us."

As they drove off as slowly and quietly as they could, Agatha muttered, "Can't you go any faster? They could be anywhere."

"They might stop suddenly and hear our engine," said Charles. "Look, I can see their lights in the distance. They've gone up that country lane. I'll follow as far as I dare."

A large barn loomed up against the night sky and the truck, and Richards stopped outside it.

"Agatha," said Charles, "before we go any further, wouldn't it be an idea to phone the police? These are stone hard killers and psychos. Think what they did to Beech."

"Just a look," pleaded Agatha, "and then we'll phone if there's anything."

They got out of the car and made their way silently towards the barn. Agatha suddenly stopped in her tracks. "I've got to pee."

"Then pee and follow us," said Charles crossly. "Couldn't you have gone all that time we were waiting behind that bloody hedge? Oh, go on."

"Wait for me," pleaded Agatha.

"I'm bored," said Charles. "I'm going to take one look and then we're off."

He and Toni crept forward, dropping down onto the grass and wriggling forward. The barn doors were open and light was streaming out.

Charles managed to get one look inside. "It's a lab," he whispered. "They must be making drugs."

And then he and Toni were seized. Toni let out a scream. Agatha, hitching up her knickers, turned and ran back to the car.

She desperately phoned the police, babbling instructions.

"How did you find us?" Richards was demanding as Toni and Charles were held captive by three men.

"Won't answer, eh? Boris, get the acetylene torch and scorch that pretty face. She'll tell us soon enough."

"It was my idea," said Charles. "The police know nothing about it."

"Well, you're going to find out what happens to snoops. Burn her face off, Boris." Charles tried to tear himself free but was held firm.

Boris advanced with the torch.

"Someone's coming!" cried Richards.

Agatha Raisin, crouched over the wheel of the Mercedes, crashed straight into the barn and right into Boris. Chemicals, glass jars and retorts went flying. She swerved and gunned the car at Richards, who leapt out of the way, but not before she had sideswiped him and broken his leg. "Shoot her!" he shouted.

Flames were beginning to flare up all round. His men were running outside for the truck.

Charles and Toni jumped into the car. Agatha reversed straight out, but the truck was driving off. "We've got to get Richards out of there," shouted Charles.

Agatha stopped. Charles ran back in and pulled Richards, who was screaming with pain, out of the inferno. His clothes were on fire, and Charles rolled him over in the grass until the flames went out.

Suddenly, there was a helicopter overhead and police sirens in the distance.

Richards had fallen unconscious. Agatha and Toni got out of the car and joined him. Toni sat down and put her head between her knees. "They were going to burn her face off, Agatha," said Charles.

Agatha sat white-faced, staring at Toni, cursing herself for her vanity that had nearly led the girl to a nasty death.

Then they were surrounded by police, ambulances and fire brigade engines.

Richards was taken off in an ambulance and under police guard. His gang had been caught.

Agatha wanted Toni to be taken to hospital to be treated for shock, but Toni refused to go.

Then they were taken off to police headquarters in Dover to be questioned before being transferred to a "safe" house to face further questioning in the morning.

The "safe" house fortunately contained nightwear and changes of clothes. They huddled together on the sofa in the small living room. Charles got up and went into the kitchen and came back with a bottle of whisky. "Look what I've found."

"Toni needs hot sweet tea," admonished Agatha.

"Toni needs to get drunk," said Toni in a weary voice.

"So it was drugs all along," said Agatha at last.

"And farm machinery and cars, probably," said Charles. "Tulloch wasn't around. I hate to think of that psycho still being on the loose."

Toni shuddered, and Agatha said quickly, "They probably got rid of him. Once he was blown, he became expendable. Let's go to bed."

During the night, Agatha woke up and found Charles in bed next to her.

"What the . . . ?"

"Just shut up and go to sleep." He put his arms around her. Agatha drifted back off to sleep into a world of nightmares, haunted by a picture of beautiful Toni's ruined face.

A policeman who had been on guard out-side the door knocked in the morning and asked them if they would like breakfast. "We'd better eat something," said Agatha.

"There's a McDonald's next door."

"Couldn't he do better than that?" grumbled Agatha.

"Nothing up with McDonald's," said Charles. "I'm starving."

They had just finished eating when they were told they were being escorted back to Mircester.

"More questioning," groaned Agatha. "What about my car?"

"You'll need to contact your insurance company. Part of the blazing barn fell on it. It's a write-off."

The three of them were interviewed separately. Toni was interviewed by Bill Wong and Alice Peterson. Somehow, as they were very gentle with her, she found it therapeutic to go through her whole story again.

When she had finished and signed her statement, Bill said, "You really must go to Victim Support."

"I'm all right now," said Toni.

"I still think you are suffering from delayed shock," said Alice. "Let me make an appointment for you."

"Very well," said Toni, feeling she would have agreed to anything just to get out of police headquarters and back to her own little flat.

Agatha and Charles met up in the reception area. "I need a shower and scrub," said Agatha. "Toni's evidently gone to her flat. Should we go and pick her up?"

"I think she'll want to be on her own for a bit," said Charles. "I couldn't get anything out of them. Has Tulloch been found?"

"Wilkes told me they're still looking for him. I don't like it. What if that psycho decides to take revenge on one of us?"

"I think he's probably long gone," said Charles, stifling a yawn.

"I should call the hospital," said Agatha, "and find out how Simon is getting on. I wonder if I should reemploy him."

"What! You must be mad. He was spying for Mixden."

"I know, I know. But look at it this way. Us amateurs have none of the resources of the police. What policeman would have the imagination to figure out what a man with a lot of money he had to keep hidden would do? Who else would think about his longing for a posh car?"

"See what Toni thinks of the idea," said Charles.

"I'm not going to do anything about it

269

now. I've got to phone my car insurance and get a courtesy car. Shall we ask the coppers to drive us back?"

"I'm sick of them," said Charles. "Let's take a taxi."

At Agatha's cottage, Charles said he would go home and maybe see her later. As she watched him drive away, Agatha felt strangely bereft and then gave herself a mental shake. Charles was like a will-o'-the-wisp, coming and going, never dependable.

Her cleaner arrived with Agatha's cats, who studiously ignored her and waited by the garden door to be let out. "You should get a cat flap," said Doris.

"What if some intruder uses it to crawl in?"

"Nobody would be that skinny enough."

"Well, they could shove a petrol bomb through it."

"They could do that through the letter-box."

"You're a barrel of laughs this morning," said Agatha, and burst into tears.

Doris looked at her in shock and then hugged her. "I'm getting Mrs. Bloxby here right now."

Mrs. Bloxby was shocked at Agatha's appearance. Usually Agatha was an advertisement for the saying that the fifties were the new forties, but she was white-faced and haggard.

After a cup of hot sweet tea laced with brandy, and two cigarettes, Agatha began to recover. "I've never seen you wearing a tracksuit before," said Mrs. Bloxby.

"Police supply from their safe house in Dover."

"I heard about it on the morning news. Of course, not much came out because of the impending court case. Tell me about it."

Mrs. Bloxby listened in horror to Agatha's tale.

"Where is Toni?" she asked.

"Back at her flat."

"And this Tulloch is still at liberty! I'm going to Mircester to get her right away."

Charles arrived home to be told by his man Gustav that Penny Dunstable was in the sitting room. Penny was one of Charles's old flames. Gustav privately thought that if he did not get Charles married off to someone suitable, then one day that Raisin female might be in residence.

Penny rose to meet him. She was tall and rangy, with square hunting shoulders, thick brown hair and a long face. Charles remembered she had been an enthusiastic lover.

"I'm done in," said Charles. "Darling Penny. Wrong day for a visit. I'm going to bed."

"Good idea," said Penny huskily.

Sex, thought Charles. Lots of it. Just what the doctor needed. Then a vision of Agatha's sad white face watching him as he left rose before his eyes. Damn Agatha.

"Sorry, darling," he said. "I'm knackered. Another time."

He walked away quickly. Gustav started to follow him up the stairs. Charles swung round. "I can put myself to bed, thank you. You invited her, didn't you?"

"I met Miss Dunstable at the farmer's market and thought you would be glad to see her."

"Not now," said Charles. "Give her a drink and get rid of her."

Toni answered the door to Mrs. Bloxby and meekly accepted an invitation to stay at the rectory. Mrs. Bloxby helped her pack. "I'm supposed to get a call from Victim Support," said Toni.

"Did you give the police your mobile phone number as well?"

"Yes."

"Then they'll be able to find you. Before

272

you leave, wouldn't you much rather be with your mother?"

"She did call, but she's just got a new job. I told her I would be all right and that I might see her at the week-end."

When they got into Mrs. Bloxby's ancient Morris Minor, the vicar's wife looked in the rearview mirror before she drove off. If only the police would come through with the news that Tulloch had been found.

She heaved a sigh of relief when she finally turned down into the tree-lined road leading to Carsely. There were no cars behind her.

Once at the vicarage, she told Toni to go and find a seat in the garden. Toni stretched out in a deck chair and felt the warm sun on her face. The peace of the vicarage garden enclosed her.

Soon she was asleep.

That evening, Agatha sealed her letterbox shut with SuperGlue, knowing the postman would leave any letters for her at the village store. She tried to phone Charles, but Gustav told her he wasn't available; but then that was what Gustav always said.

She went up to the landing and looked longingly at James's cottage, but no light showed and his car was not parked outside.

The doorbell rang, making her jump nervously. She went down the stairs and looked through the spy hole. Bill Wong's face stared back. Agatha opened the door.

"Come in. Has he been caught?"

"Who?"

"Tulloch, of course."

"We're working on that. We might get one of the gang to talk soon. One of them seems weaker than the others. We're hoping to hear that Richards got rid of him. We're winding up the whole business. Imagine having a successful chain of supermarkets and that not being enough. The drug lab was to be a new venture, all set up to make crystal meth, as far as forensic could gather from the burnt-out remains. Where is Toni?"

"Staying with Mrs. Bloxby."

"The best thing she could do."

"She would have been quite safe with me," said Agatha huffily.

"Let's hope you're not in any danger," said Bill, looking at the bars on the kitchen window.

Agatha followed his gaze and said bitterly, "I'm in a sort of prison when Tulloch may be out there, roaming free. Hey, what about Fiona Richards? Did she know anything about all this?"

"She denies it vehemently and tearfully.

All she can wonder about is what is going to happen to her previously expensive life-style."

"And is Richards really the head of things?"

"Before his ambition to join the drug market, it was pinching cars and expensive farm machinery and shipping it to Eastern Europe. In the men we picked up, there were two Albanians, one Kurd, and I regret to say two residents of Mircester, the latter both having spent time in prison in the past for grievous bodily harm."

Bill's phone rang. He walked out of the kitchen to answer it. When he came back, his face was grim. "One of the gang has started to sing. He says that Beech would earn money by telling Richards which combine harvesters were left out on the fields and where to pick up expensive cars. Maybe the P in his ledger was for Porsche. He also tipped Richards off when it looked as if one of the gang might be under suspicion and managed to 'lose' the evidence. But he felt he wasn't getting enough and started to blackmail Richards. Richards ordered a man called Boris Ahmid and one of the Englishmen, Marty Gifford, to deal with Beech in such a way as to frighten off anyone else who might want to play the same trick. The roast pig idea was Boris's. The missing feet and arms have been found in a freezer at the back of the main supermarket store in Mircester."

"Wouldn't one of the staff have found them?"

"It was a padlocked freezer. Richards is a sick and vicious man. The rest of his gang are soon going to turn against him when they learn he's going to plead that they threatened him into doing their dirty work."

"And when did Tulloch enter the picture?"

"I think shortly after Beech's murder. He's a compulsive gambler and owed money to a loan shark. Richards heard about it through the loan shark. We believe Tulloch drugged himself outside Agatha's cottage to divert suspicion from himself.

"Tulloch killed Amy Richards. She was about to take over the blackmailing. How on earth the silly woman thought she could get away with it is beyond me."

"But what is Tulloch's record?"

"Seemed straightforward copper until we started digging. His wife called us out one night. She had been beaten. Two broken ribs. Then she withdrew the charge. But it left a nasty taste in the mouth. He divorced her a few months later. He was transferred to us from Manchester. Now, before he left

Manchester there had been a series of brutal, sadistic murders of prostitutes. After he left, nothing. Makes you think."

Simon could not sleep that night. He was recovering rapidly, but not in spirit. He had never felt so low or so shamed in all his life. He was sure the army had seen through his fake post-traumatic stress but after his treatment of Sue had decided it would be better just to get rid of him. His parents knew all about his spying for Mixden and looked at him sadly, as if they could not believe they had created such a monster.

There had been a police guard outside his door, but when he had been considered strong enough to move to a general ward, the police guard had been taken off. The fact that his parents had not seen fit to pay for a private room for him had shaken him.

Sometimes, in his lowest moments, he began to wish he really had died. And yet it was his fear of Tulloch returning to finish the job that kept him alert, had made him refuse the sleeping pills.

The other patients did not talk to him. He had heard one say, "He's probably a criminal."

He was thankful he now had enough strength to go to the bathroom himself without enduring the indignity of ringing for a bedpan. He emerged from the bathroom and hesitated, wondering whether to see if he could get any food from the kitchen. Soup and a sandwich had been served at six o'clock in the evening, and he knew he could not expect more food until the following morning. The night nurse was not at her desk. He managed to find a small kitchen outside the ward and made himself a cup of coffee and a cheese sandwich. Beginning to feel a bit weak and shaky, he cautiously emerged from the kitchen to make his way back to his bed. In front of him was what looked at first like a hospital orderly pushing a trolley of medicine. The orderly stopped outside Simon's ward, selected a syringe and filled it. Simon began to shake with fear. There was something horribly familiar about that burly figure with the fair hair. He retreated slowly and then began to run until he reached the main desk, crying, "Get the police. It's Tulloch. He's trying to murder me!"

Soon the hospital was surrounded. In the abandoned cart, they found a syringe full of cyanide. Bill Wong, hurrying to the hospital, wondered if he would ever get a decent night's sleep again. But Tulloch — and it must have been Tulloch, for who else would want to kill Simon? — had disappeared.

Simon was once more removed to a private room with a policeman on guard outside. He had a sudden longing for the abrasive person of Agatha Raisin.

Agatha was awakened by the shrill ringing of the phone by her bedside. She squinted at the clock. Three in the morning? She picked up the phone.

"It's me, Simon," the voice on the other end whispered. "Don't hang up."

"What do you want, you sneaky little toad?" demanded Agatha.

"Tulloch's been here at the hospital." He rapidly told her what had happened, ending up by saying, "I need to see you."

"God knows why," said Agatha acidly. "Look, you're no longer in intensive care, I gather. So I'll be along in the morning when they allow visitors."

She slept uneasily for the rest of the night. Every rustle in the thatched roof made her think of Tulloch crawling up there; every creak from the old timbers made her think he was trying to find a way in.

I have never been this frightened for so long, thought Agatha miserably. Oh, for the boring life of lost teenagers and cats back again. I swear I'll never complain.

Agatha took her time getting to the hospital. She went to Achille in Evesham to get her hair done before going to see Simon.

Simon saw her approach through the open door of his room and called to the policeman on guard to let her in.

"Glad to see you're looking stronger," said Agatha gruffly. "But I can now tell you, you are one sneaky piece of work."

"I'm sorry," said Simon. His thick hair was ruffled up, and he looked very young. "The fact is I'm terrified. Every doctor who enters the room makes me shiver. It's going to be one horror of a night ahead."

"How did you leap to the conclusion that one bent copper would try to buy an expensive car?" asked Agatha.

"It's the sort of thing I thought he might do. Most chaps who win the lottery, well, the first thing they want is a flashy car."

Boys and their toys, thought Agatha. "If only we could catch him," she said, half to herself. "He's one mad psycho."

"I've an awful feeling he'll try again," said Simon.

Agatha looked at him thoughtfully. She was tired of the police treating her like a bumbling amateur when they wouldn't even have found the drugs factory if it hadn't been for her.

"I see you've got a private bathroom," she said.

"Want to use it?"

"No, not now. See, it's like this. All Tulloch has to do to get at you again is put on a white coat and look like a doctor."

"There's a police guard outside."

"That wouldn't matter if Tulloch disguises himself a bit, pinches some doctor's outfit and name tag. Quick stab in your arm with a syringe and it's goodbye, Simon, hullo, psycho."

"I wish you hadn't come," said Simon. "I didn't think it was possible to be any more frightened than I am, but you've just proved it's possible."

"Listen! I'll come back here towards the end of visiting hour. You distract the copper by calling him to the window and saying you thought you saw Tulloch outside in the grounds. I'll nip into the bathroom and stay there for the night on guard."

"Agatha! Tulloch is as strong as an ox. You'd never be able to overpower him, and he'd probably have dealt with that poor policeman."

"Don't you worry about that."

"You're crazy!"

281

"Then lie there and tremble for all I care."

"Okay," said Simon reluctantly. "I can do with all the protection I can get."

Agatha went from the hospital to her office. She did not plan to tell any of them or Charles of her plans. If anyone was going to be put in danger, then it would be herself.

Toni was still resting at the vicarage. She gave Phil and Patrick a few jobs to clear up, dictated letters to Mrs. Freedman and then said she felt a bit shaky and would go home and rest.

Just before the end of visiting hours, she arrived carrying a large bag containing two flasks of coffee and a packet of sandwiches. At her signal, Simon called to the policeman that he thought he had just seen Tulloch. The policeman came rushing in to join him at the window, and Agatha nipped into the bathroom and closed the door.

Simon came in later to clean his teeth. "It may have backfired. All that happened was that there were police all over the hospital for most of the evening."

"There are four police guards at the entrance," said Agatha.

"Good," said Simon. "Now, I have to pee."

"I'll turn my back and promise not to

peek," said Agatha, "and keep your voice down."

The night wore on. Agatha drank cup after cup of coffee, willing herself to stay awake. Sometimes she could hear footsteps in the corridor outside and stiffened, waiting. She longed to be able to go outside and check if the policeman was still alert and on guard. There should have been two of them, she thought. What if he wanted to go to the loo? Her heart sank. The intelligent thing would be to use the loo in Simon's bathroom.

Her eyes were just beginning to droop when she heard voices outside. She opened the bathroom door a crack.

"Thought you'd never get here," she heard what she recognised as the policeman's voice say. "I'm knackered. Don't recognise you. You're not from headquarters."

"Over from Worcester," she heard another voice say. "They're drafting us in from all over."

Agatha trembled. Didn't that new voice have a slight Scottish burr?

Simon was fast asleep. How could he sleep in the middle of all this? thought Agatha angrily.

She kept the door open a crack. A man in police uniform was cautiously approaching the bed where Simon lay. And then, horrified, Agatha saw the glimpse of a syringe in his hand. She seized a porcelain bedpan and crept up behind him. As he gently pulled up the sleeve of Simon's hospital nightgown, Agatha smashed the bedpan down on the back of his head.

Simon woke up with a scream. Agatha bent down and heaved the now unconscious man over. Tulloch! Footsteps could be heard racing along the corridor, and suddenly the room was full of policemen.

"It's Tulloch!" said Agatha. "I hope I haven't killed him."

Tulloch groaned and tried to sit up. A hospital trolley was brought in, and he was handcuffed to it and wheeled away for treatment.

It transpired that the policeman who had left thinking his tour of duty was over had told the police at the entrance to the hospital that he had been replaced by a man from Worcester. He was told he was supposed to be replaced by a policeman from Mircester, and they had all rushed back up to Simon's room in time to find Agatha holding a bedpan and Tulloch on the floor.

EPILOGUE

Agatha Raisin was not a heroine. That was borne firmly in on her by Inspector Wilkes. She was not to talk to the press because it was all sub judice until the court case was over.

In vain did she point out that if it hadn't been for her intervention, Simon would be dead. As she wearily left police headquarters the following morning, she thought about calling the media and leaking the story but decided against it. A really angry police force might start to interfere in her business, and she needed their goodwill.

All that appeared on television that day and in the newspapers on the following day was that a man had been arrested and charged with the attempted murder of Simon Black.

But it couldn't be kept quiet. A male nurse told his friend about Agatha hiding in the bathroom and braining Tulloch with a bedpan, so the gossip swirled round and onto the reporting desks of the local newspapers.

Stories about Agatha began to appear in the press. She diplomatically replied that she could not say anything until after the court case.

Five days after her adventure, Bill Wong came to tell her that Tulloch was suing her for grievous bodily harm. "He can't do that!" wailed Agatha.

"Get yourself a lawyer. He won't get away with it, but we have to go through the motions, not to mention the miles and miles of paperwork. How are you feeling?"

"Relieved. I can get my old life back. Work has been suffering because of all this Tulloch business."

"Where's Charles?"

"I thought he would be round, but I haven't heard from him. Roy is due to arrive. He feels he's missing out on a bit of free publicity. What about you and Alice?"

Bill actually blushed. "They don't like staff getting together. I'd like to ask her out, but she might refuse. She values her job and wouldn't want to put it in jeopardy."

"Look at my cats, crawling all over you!" exclaimed Agatha. "The only signs of affection I get from them are when they want food."

"I'm sure they're fond of you. Is that someone at the door?"

It was Roy, resplendent in a white cotton suit, striped shirt and silk tie. His hair was conventionally cut.

"Who are you representing?" asked Agatha. "Someone conventional?"

"No, it's a new boy band called the Irreproachable. They dress square, so I'm supposed to fit in."

"You look good."

"I'm off," said Bill. "See you in court."

Once he had taken his overnight bag up to the spare room, Roy demanded to know all the details.

"Let's sit in the garden," said Agatha. "The weather's lovely."

"You need a gardener," commented Roy. "It's a jungle."

"Do you know," said Agatha, "I've been frightened to engage someone in case it should turn out to be Tulloch or someone from the gang. I'll get someone now."

"So tell me all about it."

How unreal it all seemed now, thought Agatha as she told him what had happened.

When she had finished, Roy asked, "How's Toni bearing up? I mean, I felt sick for ages after my kidnapping, but, I mean, thinking you're going to get your face burnt off!"

"She's been getting counselling and she seems to be all right. It's hard to tell with Toni. She'd been staying at the vicarage, but she went back to her flat as soon as she heard about Tulloch's arrest. Do you know Tulloch is suing me for grievous bodily harm?"

"He won't get away with it, surely?"

"It's up to the Crown Prosecution Service, but in the meantime, I'd better get my lawyer onto it. You know, I'm almost tempted to ask Simon back."

"What! To work for you after he was prepared to sneak on your work to Mixden?"

"Well . . . I know. It's just he's such a good detective. You see, I need someone with intuition. We don't have the same resources as the police."

"But what if he works for you and takes a payoff from Mixden? And what about dumping that girl at the altar? What about chickening out of the army?"

"The girl tricked him by saying she was pregnant. I don't know that I blame him for not wanting to go back. It seems that Sergeant Sue is highly popular in the regiment, and Simon got really trashed in the

288

local papers for dumping her at the altar. Also, Mixden's in trouble with the police. They're trying to charge him with industrial espionage or something, but it's his word against Simon's and nobody wants to believe a word Simon says anymore."

"And what about Toni?"

Agatha looked singularly shifty. "I'll have to ask her."

Roy rose to his feet. "I'll just run up to the vicarage and have a talk with Mrs. Bloxby."

"Wait! I'll come with you."

"I'd like a chat with her on my own. She's better than any therapist."

"Oh, go," said Agatha huffily.

When Roy had left, Agatha sat miserably staring at the kitchen table. She suddenly felt very much alone. One of her cats, Boswell, jumped on her lap and stared into her face, and Hodge, the other, climbed up her back and draped itself round her neck.

A tear rolled down Agatha's face. "You wretched animals. You care after all!"

Roy was away for an hour. At times Agatha thought of simply leaving and abandoning him for the rest of the day.

Toni's doorbell rang. Simon's voice came through the intercom. "Can I come up?"

"I suppose so," said Toni reluctantly, and let him in.

"You still look a bit white," she said when Simon walked into the room. "When did they let you out?"

"This morning." He sat down wearily in an armchair.

"And why are you here?"

"I couldn't think of anywhere to go."

"Aren't you living with your parents?"

"They got me a flat. They keep looking at me with such disappointment in their eyes, I can't bear it."

"I can understand them," said Toni. "I went for a job at Mixden because I thought Agatha had driven you into the army. When he suggested I spy on her, I walked out. Agatha can be infuriating and meddling, but I owe her a lot."

"I wish I could work for her again. I mean, if I hadn't had that flash of genius about searching car salesrooms, maybe no one would have got on to Tulloch."

"Simon! She wouldn't even have you gift-wrapped. And you said how much you hated working for her!"

"I know. But she did save my life. Maybe the reason she annoys me is because there's a good bit of Agatha in me."

He leaned forward. "Look, Toni, just suppose she did say yes, what would you feel about it?"

"Do you mean romantically or professionally?"

"Professionally."

"I don't know. I would like someone of my own age around. I seem to have got divorced from all my old school friends. I'm the odd girl out. I don't like binge drinking. They like to go to clubs on a Saturday night and get wasted."

"Nobody loves me either," said Simon gloomily.

"Yeah. But you deserve it."

"Fancy going to a movie?"

"What kind of movie?"

"There's a rerun of *Gigi* at the Classic. But you've probably seen it."

"No," said Toni. "That's one I missed."

"Come one, then. Great musical. Great fun. What else were you planning to do?"

"All right. But don't get any ideas!"

"None. I promise. I'm off women."

"I'll just get my bag."

Roy returned in high good humour. "I've got a surprise for you."

"What now?" asked Agatha. Her cats slid off her and disappeared into the long grass of the garden.

"I've found someone to do your garden."

"Big deal. Look, I'm grateful. But I could have found someone myself. Who is this fellow? Or is it a woman?"

"No, he's just moved into the village."

"Gnarled and creaking?"

"Gorgeous. I'm telling you, babes, he's to die for."

"How did you meet this paragon?"

"I happened to mention to Mrs. Bloxby that your garden was a mess."

"Oh, really? Was that part of your *therapy* session?"

"It was after we'd had our little talk. Don't get bitchy."

"I," said Agatha Raisin, "am *never* bitchy."

"Yes, well, never mind that," said Roy hurriedly. "Mrs. Bloxby happened to mention that there was an incomer, George Marston, who does gardens. He lives in a cottage at the village end. The one called Wisteria Cottage."

"Didn't old Mrs. Henry live there?"

"You really are out of touch. She died last year. So I went there and this Adonis answered the door. He says he does gardening and all sorts of odd jobs."

"What age?"

"Hard to tell. Not young. Maybe early forties. Posh accent."

Agatha winced. Early forties seemed young to her.

"So why is this posh-accented beauty offering himself as a labourer?"

"Why don't you phone him and ask him? Come on, Aggie. Just look at your garden."

"Oh, all right. What's the number?"

"Here's his card."

Agatha phoned. The cultured voice at the other end said he would be along in a few minutes.

"Can't be getting that much work if he's so eager," she said. "The sun is over the yardarm or whatever. I'm going to have a gin and tonic. What about you?"

"I'll have the same."

They sat over their drinks in the garden. It was a beautiful Cotswold day, with fleecy clouds drifting against a dark blue sky.

There came a ring at the doorbell. Roy shot to his feet. "I'll get it!"

Agatha waited, suddenly glad of the diversion.

Roy entered the garden followed by a tall man. Agatha was wearing sunglasses. She took them off and stared at the vision before her.

George Marston was over six feet tall, with thick grey blond hair and green eyes in a square, tanned face. His body under his dress of chinos and sweatshirt looked muscular.

Agatha rose to her feet. "Roy, get Mr. Marston a drink. I have to go upstairs."

Putting on an extra layer of make-up, thought Roy.

Agatha scrubbed off her make-up and carefully applied a new layer. She slipped out of the loose cotton dress she had been wearing and changed into a gingham blouse, tight jeans and wedge-heeled sandals. She looked in the mirror. Country but sexy, she thought with satisfaction. There was a lot to be said for fear and misery. One lost weight. She went back downstairs.

"Now, Mr. Marston . . . ."

"George, please."

"George. I run a detective agency and recently have been under threat, so don't think me rude if I ask you a lot of questions."

He smiled. Agatha's heart gave a lurch. "Fire away," he said.

"First of all, what is your background?"

"I was in the army."

"For how long?"

"Twenty years."

"When did you leave?"

"Eight months ago."

"May I ask why?"

"Certainly." He rolled up his left trouser leg, showing an artificial limb. "Present from Afghanistan," he said.

"How awful," said Agatha.

"It's all right. I've got used to it. I'm good at all sorts of things — carpentry, gardening, things like that."

"Well, I see no reason why you don't join me for a drink and then you can start right away. What are your rates?"

"Eight pounds an hour."

"I feel obliged to tell you that the going rate in Carsely is ten pounds an hour."

"To be frank," he said, "I need the work and thought I would get it if I were a little bit cheaper."

"We'll see how you go," said Agatha. "If your work is okay, you can earn the going rate. Now, what would you like to drink?"

"Is that gin and tonic? I'd like one of those. I see an ashtray on the table. Mind if I smoke?"

"Of course not. I smoke myself. Roy, be an angel and get George a drink."

When Roy had gone indoors, George settled in a chair and said, "Isn't that the young man who was kidnapped?"

"Yes. The whole thing has been frightening and I'm just getting over it."

"Tell me about it."

So Agatha did, while Roy returned with George's drink and then sat in sulky silence, feeling he was being ignored.

"You've certainly been through the wars," he said when Agatha had finished. "Look, if you don't mind, I'll get started."

"The gardening things and the mower are all in the shed at the bottom of the garden," said Agatha. "I'll show you."

He worked all week-end. Roy complained that he had been ignored because Agatha could hardly bear to leave the house, preferring to sit out in the garden and admire her new acquisition.

"Don't fall for him," warned Roy when he left. "I mean, what a cliché!"

"What are you talking about?"

"Middle-aged woman lusts after gardener."

"Don't be silly."

When Agatha returned to her cottage, she had an impulse to invite George out for dinner. If Charles had turned up or if James had returned home, she would have decided against it. But she felt lonely.

The garden was being rapidly restored. George was putting away the tools in the shed when Agatha called to him, "Like a drink?"

"A cold beer would be lovely if you have one."

Agatha found one at the back of the fridge and filled a glass.

"Are you married?" asked Agatha.

"I was once. Don't want to talk about it."

"Children?"

"No. Let's talk about the garden. It won't take me long to get it in shape for the autumn." He drained his glass. Agatha paid him. "Isn't this too much?" he asked.

"No, your work is good, so you get the going rate."

"If I keep the shed keys, then I can get into the garden by the path at the side of the house and I won't need to disturb you."

"That's fine. I've got a spare set. I'll be out at work," said Agatha, "but I might drop home during the day to see how you are getting on."

"Fine," said George. Then he rose easily from his seat, waved to her and moved swiftly away. Agatha winced as she heard the front door shut behind him.

But she was not to be left alone for long. As she went to answer the summons of the doorbell, she thought with relief that it was simply marvellous to be able to answer her own front door without a feeling of terror.

Simon stood there, looking plaintively at her.

"Oh, it's you," said Agatha. "What do you want?"

"I wondered if you could ever see your way to giving me another chance?"

"Oh, come in."

"Your garden looks better," said Simon. "Have you been working on it?"

"Yes," said Agatha, all at once wanting to keep the glory of finding George to herself. "Take a seat, Simon, and tell me why I should ever trust you again. What made you volunteer to spy for Mixden?"

"I was pretty sure that after the wedding, you wouldn't consider having me back. I know I'm good at detecting."

"I can't have you back," said Agatha. "Toni would never forgive me, for a start. It was she you used to winkle out information."

"She says she will."

"When? How?"

"I had a talk with her and we went to the movies."

"Look, I could certainly do with someone with your intuition. But it's not only Toni I have to consider. It's Phil, Patrick and Mrs. Freedman. I'll discuss it with them tomorrow. If I do take you back, you will need to work at all the lowest jobs for two months until I feel I can trust you. You will also need to sign a confidentiality document, and if you sneak to Mixden, I'll sue your socks off."

On Monday morning, Agatha told her staff about Simon. Phil was all for giving him another chance, Toni said she did not mind, but Mrs. Freedman and Patrick said he had proved himself untrustworthy. But when Agatha started to look at all the cases she had neglected, and they all realised there was a lot of hard work ahead, Patrick reluctantly said it would be useful to have someone to do the lost cats and dogs kind of work.

Mrs. Freedman said that in that case she would go along with it.

A two-month trial was decided on, and Agatha phoned Simon.

Three more cases came in that morning, and Agatha, who had hoped to rush off early and maybe see George, found she had to work long hours.

Mrs. Ada Benson called on Mrs. Bloxby. The vicar's wife looked at her wearily. "What now?" she asked.

"Dear me," said Mrs. Benson. "One would think I was always complaining. It's just a little matter."

Mrs. Bloxby reluctantly stood aside, and Mrs. Benson walked into the sitting room.

"It's like this," she began. "There is a newcomer in this village. A Mr. George Marston."

"Yes, I know," said Mrs. Bloxby. "What about him?"

"He appears to be working full-time for Mrs. Raisin."

"So? I know he needs work."

"But he should be warned."

"What on earth are you talking about?"

"Agatha Raisin is a *man-eater!*"

Mrs. Bloxby sighed. "Would you please leave, Mrs. Benson, and in future, would you telephone first? I am very busy. Please shut the door on your way out."

"Well, I never!"

"Then it's time you did. Goodbye!"

Agatha longed for the week-end. The weather was still golden. Cotswold cottages lazed under a warm sun. Often, when they were busy, she and her staff would work on Saturdays as well, but she told them firmly that the following week-end was to be free — with the exception of Simon, who was asked to continue trying to find a missing teenager.

She was up early on Saturday, trying on one outfit after another, settling at last for a white cotton blouson, blue cotton skirt and high-heeled sandals.

He was already in the garden when she descended.

"Coffee?" she called out.

"Fine."

When she had two mugs of coffee ready, he joined her at the garden table.

"Did you bring your bill?" asked Agatha.

He pulled a piece of paper from his pocket. Agatha opened her handbag, took out her wallet and paid him the amount.

"I've cost you a lot of money," he said, "but as you can see, everything's nearly finished. In fact, I'll be finished at lunchtime. Of course, I'll be back occasionally to mow the lawn and do the weeding. I've been lucky to land several other jobs."

"The garden looks lovely. I didn't realise I had so many flowers," said Agatha, who could not remember the name of even one of them. "I say, this demands a celebration. Why don't I take you for lunch today?"

"That would be nice. I'll go home and change first. What time?"

"We'll leave here at twelve thirty."

"Right. I'll get back to work."

I must play it cool, thought Agatha. She went indoors and phoned a restaurant in Broadway that she knew had tables outside and made a booking for one o'clock.

Charles Fraith had put off contacting Agatha. He was feeling increasingly drawn to her, and he did not like to be emotionally involved with anyone. That Saturday, he decided it would do no harm just to call in and see her. But in the morning, another former girlfriend called on him and he found himself asking her out for lunch instead. She was called Rosamund and was dainty and pretty, not at all like Agatha. But Agatha always exuded a strong air of sensuality of which she seemed completely unaware.

Agatha was almost ready to leave when the phone rang. It was Mrs. Bloxby. "I'm in a rush," said Agatha. She giggled. "I'm taking the new gardener to Russell's in Broadway for lunch."

"How kind of you," said Mrs. Bloxby, repressing a desire to shriek down the line, "Not again! Do be careful."

She said she would call her later.

■ ■ ■ ■

James Lacey arrived home and flipped through his accumulated post. He put all the bills and circulars to one side. There was one letter for him with a handwritten address. He opened it up. It was from Roy. "Dear James," he read, "Our Agatha has fallen for her gardener. You know what she's like and the trouble she's got into in the past by falling for unsuitable men. She knows nothing about this one. Do check up on her. Your dear friend, Roy."

James was tempted to forget about it, but Agatha had put herself in danger in the past. He went next door, but Agatha's cottage was empty. He phoned Mrs. Bloxby and asked her if she knew where Agatha was.

"Mrs. Raisin has taken her new gardener for lunch at Russell's in Broadway," said Mrs. Bloxby, "but she should be back home later today."

James thanked her and rang off. Then he decided it would do no harm just to go to Broadway and have a look at this fellow.

Agatha was enjoying herself. George did not talk much but seemed amused and interested in Agatha's highly colourful description of the cases she had worked on.

They had just reached the coffee stage when a long shadow fell across their table.

"Hullo, Agatha."

"James!" cried Agatha. "Just passing by?" she added hopefully.

"May I join you for a coffee?"

"All right," said Agatha in a voice that meant she did not think it was all right one little bit. She made the introductions.

"Lacey!" exclaimed George. "Not Colonel Lacey?"

"I'm retired now," said James, sitting down.

"I read your book on military logistics when I was at Sandhurst," said George.

"I've got it. George Marston. Major George Marston. I read about you," said James. "What a hero. You rescued four of your men before you got your foot blown off. How are you doing?"

"I had to have a whole prosthetic leg from the knee down," said George. "I manage. How did you meet Agatha?"

"I live next door and I'm her ex-husband. I hear you're doing a bit of gardening."

"As much as I can get."

"I'm right next door to Agatha. You're welcome to do mine. I usually do it myself, but I haven't had the time."

"I'll have a look at yours after lunch," said George.

"Tell me about Afghanistan," said James. "Are we ever going to get out of there?"

"I don't know," said George. "But I'll tell you what it was like in Helmund before I left."

Agatha smoked and watched the passing crowds of tourists, feeling forgotten and outside this masculine world of war. And why did James have to come butting in? Their voices rose and fell, naming names of people Agatha did not know. At last George turned to her apologetically and said, "I am so sorry. We must be boring you to death."

"Not at all," said Agatha. "How did you find me, James?"

"Mrs. Bloxby told me where you were. I've been reading bits about you in the papers. You must have been having an awful time of it. Why don't I take you out for dinner tonight and we can talk about it?"

"Sorry, James," said Agatha. "I've got work to catch up on at home."

James looked surprised and taken aback, remembering the days when Agatha would have jumped at an invitation from him. It was a good thing George had turned out to be all right. Agatha was obviously in the grip of one of her obsessions.

"Are you still working on Agatha's jungle?" he asked.

"Just about finished," said George, "apart from a bit of maintenance."

"Finished your lunch?" said James. "I'll follow you back and show you my garden."

At James's cottage, Agatha longed to follow them in but did not want to appear too pushy. Men could smell needy across two continents, she thought bitterly.

Charles turned up on her doorstep in the early evening. "You can't stay," said Agatha quickly.

"Why?"

"I've brought a lot of work home from the office and I don't want to be disturbed."

"May I have a drink before you push me out?"

"Okay. What?"

"Whisky and water."

"Right. Take a seat in the garden."

Agatha realised as she returned with the drinks that she should never have allowed Charles into the garden.

"The place looks beautiful," he said. "Got a new gardener?"

"Yes."

"What's he like?"

"Oh, the usual. Grumpy and old, but he does good work."

Charles found Agatha's conversation practically monosyllabic and finally got up to leave. "See you soon," he said.

"Phone first!" said Agatha sharply.

"Come on, Aggie. Who is he?"

"I don't know what you're talking about."

"It's Saturday. You're perfectly made up and that must be the shortest skirt in your wardrobe, not to mention the highest heels."

"You're being silly. Just go."

Charles was getting into his car when he noticed James standing talking to an extremely handsome man. He strolled over. James made the introductions. "We're both old army men," said James, "and we've been talking most of the day. George has moved into the village. He's done Agatha's garden and he's going to do mine."

"Really?" said Charles. "Now, that is interesting."

"Why?" asked George.

"Oh, nothing." But Charles exchanged a speaking glance with James. It looked as if Agatha was heading for one of her obsessions.

As soon as he had gone, Agatha kicked off her high heels and wriggled her toes. She must make more work for George. He said he did carpentry.

She went upstairs and put on a pair of sneakers, shorts and an old shirt blouse. Then she went downstairs and out into the garden, her cats scampering after her. In the shed, she took out a heavy sledgehammer and a saw and then returned to her sitting room, leaving the cats shut out in the garden.

In her sitting room, along one wall, was a set of wooden bookshelves. She carefully began to take down all the books and pile them on the floor. Then she attacked the shelves with the sledgehammer. They had been well made and she was exhausted by the time she had reduced only half of them to splintered piles of timber.

A ring at the doorbell made her start guiltily. She firmly shut the sitting room door and answered the front door. "Oh, Mrs. Bloxby," said Agatha. "What's up?"

"Just a social call. You look all hot and dusty."

"Just clearing out some old books. Come in. Go through to the garden and I'll bring you a sherry."

"It's turned a bit cold," said Mrs. Bloxby.

"Then go to the kitchen," snapped Agatha, wishing she hadn't let her friend in.

But her car was outside, and if Mrs. Bloxby had not received any reply, she would have started to worry.

Agatha came back with a glass of sherry. "I'll be back in a moment. I've got to wash my hands. Sorry. Should have done that before I served you sherry, but it's just paper dust."

Mrs. Bloxby waited until Agatha had gone upstairs. She looked through the open door of the kitchen to the firmly closed door of the sitting room. Why had Mrs. Raisin looked so *furtive?*

On impulse, she moved quietly across the hall and opened the sitting room door. She gazed in horror at the mess, at the splintered and shattered bookshelves, before retreating quickly to the kitchen.

She remembered that George Marston had put up a notice in the local shop announcing he did carpentry as well as gardening.

Oh, Mrs. Raisin, thought Mrs. Bloxby sadly, the things you do for love. And where is this obsession going to lead?

ABOUT THE AUTHOR

M. C. Beaton was born in Scotland and lives with her husband in a village in the English Cotswolds. She writes mysteries featuring Agatha Raisin and Hamish Macbeth, as well as an Edwardian detective series published under the name Marion Chesney. Ms. Beaton is also a film commentator on BBC television.

We hope you have enjoyed this Large Print book. Other Thorndike, Wheeler, Kennebec, and Chivers Press Large Print books are available at your library or directly from the publishers.

For information about current and upcoming titles, please call or write, without obligation, to:

Publisher
Thorndike Press
10 Water St., Suite 310
Waterville, ME 04901
Tel. (800) 223-1244

or visit our Web site at:

http://gale.cengage.com/thorndike

OR

Chivers Large Print
published by AudioGO Ltd
St James House, The Square
Lower Bristol Road
Bath BA2 3SB
England
Tel. +44(0) 800 136919
email: info@audiogo.co.uk
www.audiogo.co.uk

All our Large Print titles are designed for easy reading, and all our books are made to last.